California Works

Stories

Dwight Holing

Jackdaw Press

California Works

Stories

New Paperback Edition

The stories in this book are works of fiction. Names, characters, places, and incidents are either products of the author's imagination or are used factiously. Any resemblance to actual persons, living or dead, is entirely coincidental.

The author acknowledges the trademarked status and trademark owners of various products referenced in this work of fiction, which have been used without permission. The publication/use of these trademarks is not authorized, associated with, or sponsored by the trademark owners.

To learn more, visit www.dwightholing.com

Follow @DwightHoling

ISBN: 978-0-9911301-8-4

DEDICATION

For Family

CONTENTS

ACKNOWLEDGMENTS

California Works: Stories is the winner of the 2012 Serena McDonald Kennedy Fiction Award and was first published by Snake Nation Press, an independent literary press located in Valdosta, Georgia. "Spines" originally appeared in the Fall 2011 issue of *Phoebe*. "Gallopers" won the 2011 *Arts & Letters* Prize for Fiction and was featured in that journal's Spring 2012 issue. A version of "Tomorrowland" was published in *Cutthroat* in Spring 2011. "Longboard" appeared in *Cutthroat's* Winter 2012 issue. A version of "Salt" was published in *Cold Mountain Review* (Spring 2012).

Cover and Author Photos by Mark Swope
www.markswopephotography.com

SPINES

The nights he rustles cactus from the national park, Borrego slips away by cutting across a dry soda lake, killing the headlights and steering by moonlight, the stars so low they mix freely with the sparkle of alkali kicking up from the Blazer's knobby tires. He cranks his window half down, just enough to keep the dust out but the desert air in, feeling the between time blow on his face, when hot and warm and cool come in alternating waves, washing over the sunless Mojave like silent surf as creatures slither, hop, and lumber awake. The musky scent of sage and oily fumes of creosote bush fill his nostrils and he breathes deep, holding the balm in as long as he can.

This night Neil Young is singing "Sugar Mountain" and Borrego is a half mile into the powdery lake bed wondering why it is the old acoustic stuff sounds better, makes more sense, when he spots a silhouette on his left, a dark cross, drooping, and not that tall. It wasn't there the night before, he's sure of it. He lets off the gas, silences the CD, and flicks on the side-mounted spotlight he uses for jacklighting mule deer. Training the powerful beam, he sees it isn't a cross, but a man. Only it isn't a man, but a boy, the kid just waiting there, standing totally still, holding his arms outstretched, his fingers spread like wingtips on a turkey vulture, his chin resting on his narrow chest, his eyes pinched shut.

The Blazer is stopped now, the motor droning and clicking, and Borrego rolls down the window the rest of the way to see if it isn't just moonshadow or his mind playing tricks. He doesn't say anything, just stares, wondering how a kid could get all the way out here, not asking himself yet who he is or what he's up to, or why.

It's the boy who speaks first. One eye opens a slit, no wider than a fringe-toed lizard's in a sandstorm, and he says, "Are you a scout?"

That surprises Borrego, not that the kid is actually talking, but if he means is he an Indian, how could he know that? Borrego's not 100 percent Cahuilla, but he's enough on his father's side to qualify to live on the rez and get a job calling out bingo numbers, not that he does either. Home is a single-wide overlooking a dry wash that fills with tumbling boulders whenever one of the infrequent but fierce storms breaks over the Little San Bernadinos and sends rainwater rushing down the rough granite slopes and into the mouth of the desert with a drunkard's thirst. In the glare of the light, Borrego sees the boy has dark hair like him, the same skin color, too, coppery like the rocks in the mountains where his father used to take him to shoot bighorn sheep, always telling him his eyes are sharper than a red tail's, his movements quieter than a sidewinder's, that he'd inherited those traits from him and they can take him far in life if he follows his path. Maybe the boy is Cahuilla, too, Borrego thinks, why he asks if he's a scout.

He swings the light to the side and the kid opens his other eye. "Which branch? Special ops? SEAL?"

Now Borrego is trying hard to make sense of it all. "What are you talking about?"

"That's okay. I know you can't answer. It's part of your survival training." The boy nods to himself, looks at the ground. "I can't feel the rumble from their treads yet, but I'm betting the tanks are on their way."

Borrego thinks maybe the kid got sunstroke, knowing people can get dehydrated in the desert even at night. He's seen it plenty of times, had it happen to himself when he'd emptied his CamelBak too soon. "How long you been standing there?"

The boy shrugs.

"Where you from?"

"Around here," the kid says, still making the cross with his arms.

Borrego takes in the surroundings, the circular basin with its drifts of salted sand lit by the moon so that it looks like one of the craters high above. Highway 62 is five miles away.

"And where's here?" He doesn't bother to swallow his growing impatience, picturing the teddy bears, pincushions, even a claret cup, stashed behind the backseat. They can get him three years, easy.

"Twentynine Palms. Sir." The boy shouts out each word. "Marine Corps Air Ground Combat Center. Sir." He gives one arm of the cross up to snap a salute.

A base brat. Borrego should've guessed. "So, what the hell you doing out here?"

"Watching live-fire training at night beats 'American Idol' by a long shot."

Borrego glances east where the distant Marine base sprawls, halogens bathing the perimeter in icy white light, green and red strobes indicating directions on the runways, blackness swallowing the sand dune training grounds that stretch halfway to Arizona.

"Your folks know where you're at?"

The boy's eyes dip to the top of his dusty shoes. It's no more than a blink, but Borrego is good at spotting the slightest movement. It's how he's never been struck by a diamondback, never been nailed by park police, or anybody else, for that matter.

"Mom's pulling night duty at Logistics Command. Dad's deployed in the Korengal. He's kicking Taliban ass. Oorah."

The boy's voice is someone else's echo, and a familiar picture starts forming in Borrego's head, the mom an admin, the old man a D.I. who grew bored training shaveheads at the

Palms following his tour in Gulf I and re-upped for a last grab at the brass ring.

"Bet he bounces a quarter off your bed when he's home," he says.

The kid stays mum, but his eyes flick at the shoe tops again. Something glistens in their corners this time and it isn't starlight. He raises his arm and resumes the cross thing. Borrego looks at the boy closely, figuring him for 11, 13 tops, begins redrawing the picture, wondering how many days it's been since they told him his dad is MIA, wonders if his mom is handling the news with a bible or bottle.

"Your old man, he told you never to take candy from a stranger, but hop in. I'll give you a lift home. It's a long walk."

When they finally hit pavement, the boy directs him through the windblown town to a treeless neighborhood past the base's main gate. Cracks spider the asphalt and potholes and old tar patches make the streets as bumpy as dirt roads. Though the streetlights are dimmed by swirling dust and most flicker and buzz like insect zappers, the houses look vaguely familiar. The rows of faded stucco two-bedrooms are standard GI issue, the front yards as brown as adobe brick and just as hard. No grass, no shrubs, no nothing grows, and Borrego, thinking the yards could use something, anything, pictures century plants, flowering acacia, maybe a blue agave or two.

The boy signals him to stop in the middle of a block and doesn't bother to say thanks for the ride or see you later as he slides out of the front seat, dashes across the street, and disappears through the front door of a darkened house. No dog barks. No lights turn on. No TV blares. Not sure why, Borrego remains parked where he is and sits for a while. He doesn't bother to turn the music on, doesn't want it to get in the way of what he's trying to listen for. He may have dozed off, he's not sure, but he's awake now when spent shocks groan and car springs squeak. An old dirt-streaked Chevy with a missing headlight eases into the driveway across the street. Borrego watches as a woman gets out. She goes inside the house where the boy went and he can see her through the window, tiredly tossing her bag on the counter, her black hair cut in a bob, taking a dishtowel, wetting it at the sink, rubbing her face. Borrego's sure now it isn't grime and fatigue she's trying to wipe off, just plain old fashioned worry and sorrow. Just the boy and her living in that dusty house now. Not even a pet tarantula or bird to help pass the time as they wait for news – good by phone, bad by a knock.

***

It's another resort brochure morning and Borrego is using a six-foot iron bar with a chisel blade to start the hole. He outlines the circumference and chunks up the crunchy top soil best he can then switches over to a round-point shovel with a smooth oak handle and begins digging in earnest, stomping the tool through the sandy gravel with his desert tan combat boot, scooping away the layers of limestone crust he'd broken apart with the iron bar, prying out the quartz-streaked chunks of granite. Like the iron bar, he keeps the shovel shiny and sharp, honed on a whetstone wheel he pedals like a bike back at the single-wide.

Borrego is thinking about the woman and boy, wondering how often he sneaks out into the desert when she works nights, does he help her with the laundry, the housecleaning now that it's just the two of them, the little time she gets off. He can feel Mrs. Walker watching him as he shovels, her pool blue eyes studying his back and shoulders moving beneath his khaki T. He doesn't have to turn around to know she's reclining on the plastic lounge positioned just so on the Baja shelf, stirring the shallow, cool water with her red-nailed fingertips, a tall glass sweating from ice cubes, grapefruit juice, and Gray Goose pulled from the poolside fridge, riding shotgun in the armrest cupholder.

By now Borrego is used to the women who own the big vacation homes in the gate-guarded communities on the other side of the park, used to their demands, their sense of entitlement, their bored flirtations. They never question where he gets the cactus and desert wildflowers he plants in their yards. Most don't negotiate over his prices even when they complain they're too high. A few usually get around to asking if he'd mind rubbing sunblock on their backs, could he take a look at the faulty lamp switch on the nightstand in the pool cabaña before he leaves.

Mrs. Walker takes a plastic surgery regular's view of her Mission-style contemporary on the 11th fairway at La Quinta. "Everything needs tightening," she'd told him his first visit. "Give that bushy bougainvillea at the entrance a Brazilian, *por favor*. That saggy pair of barrel cactus could use a *mucho* tuck and lift." When she smiles nothing creases or wrinkles.

Borrego had to remind her right then and there he doesn't do mow and blow. To underscore the point he told he would frame the walkway with ocotillo at $200 a pop, telling her how the flowers look like tubes of lipsticks when they bloom, thinking she'll probably coordinate her nail polish with them. He told her he'd plant a custom cactus garden, too, only cholla, all rare. "Nothing jumping," is what he'd said, not bothering to explain that cholla really didn't do that, just broke off the same as seeds do in a desert wind, hitchhiking on whatever passed too close, a kid who strayed off the nature trail, a Labradoodle escaped the leash, the woman chasing after it.

"Mr. Walker want anything special?" he'd asked.

She would've winked if the lids weren't so tight. "Gerald wouldn't notice if I asked you for a yucca in the middle of our bedroom. The only time he stays here is when he's invited a client over to play 18, have the Petrale sole at the club afterward."

Now Borrego finishes digging the hole and grips the pale green cholla with spines the color of Mrs. Walker's just-so tousled hair with his thick brown leather gloves, one hand cupping the shallow root ball, the other holding the slender trunk, and firmly guides it in, toeing the dirt in as he does.

"What kind is it?" she calls from her end of the pool.

"Wolf's," he says, telling her to be careful when it blooms, not to be fooled into trying to smell the bronze-petaled cups with the red filaments that wave like sea anemones. "The little gray and white bird with black stripes flies around here, the loggerhead shrike? Size of a sparrow, but the heart of a hawk? It impales lizards on the spines to hold them while he rips them apart."

Like always, shudders in the pool make ripples and the azure water wrinkles.

***

It's an hour-and-half drive back around the national park to the single-wide and Borrego is listening to another track from the old Young album now, trying to remember all the words, why it's the only one he plays now, counting the number of plants he'll need to complete Mrs. Walker's garden, wondering if he'll run into the kid again if he goes rustling later that night. He tries to recall who is next on the list: The gay couple who wants a pair of saguaros erected at the backdoor of the Palm Springs place once owned by Sinatra? The horseowner who ordered a meadow of goldfields, apricot mallow, and indigo bush to spice up her beige-on-beige *rancho* in Indian Wells?

The money is getting easier, that's for sure, and the days since he got back and was forced to eat cactus before figuring out he could sell it are getting further and further away. He still hunts chuckwalla, though, the tasty foot-and-half-long lizards that hide in rock crevices and balloon themselves up to make it hard to pry them out. He likes to cook them where he kills them, rub them in sage and roast them on a spit over a bed of mesquite embers. And after he eats, likes to close his eyes and fall asleep right there, his dreaming under the stars not of deserts where people are shooting at whatever moves and blowing each other up with homemade bombs sewed inside dead dogs left on the side of the road, but of quiet pools of spring water hidden in the shadows of narrow slickrock canyons and forests full of cholla that bloom only at night.

Borrego stops to pick up a six-pack at the Chevron station, downing the first can while it's still cold as he passes by the line of trucker motels that glow like a string of half burned out Christmas tree bulbs alongside 62, turns off the highway onto the oiled gravel road that crosses the bajada and up toward his place. Has the second beer going as he turns up an even bumpier dirt road walled in on both sides by smoke trees and cat's claw that grow between boulders lapped by waves of sand. The sun has already set and the spine of the bony mountains just beyond are letting go of the reflection, the pinks and reds slipping into plum and navy. Pale stars emerge in the heavens as he pulls up to the trailer and sees the kid hunching inside a too-big USMC sweatshirt at the picnic table.

"I didn't tell you where I lived," Borrego says, shutting the Blazer's door behind him. He dangles the four remaining cans by a finger hooked through one of the empty plastic rings. "I didn't even tell you my name."

The kid just says, "How come you keep all those quails and doves locked up in the cage back there? You got a desert tortoise in a horse trough full of sand, too. Don't you know it's an endangered species, protected by law?"

"Not in any danger of getting crushed by a dune buggy in there, is he? You didn't answer my question. How did you find me?"

The kid gestures at the faded white refrigerator standing outside the trailer, a heavy duty orange extension cord poking through a crank window missing a louver. "I saw the hotdogs, but no ketchup. Where do you keep the buns?"

Borrego drops what remains of the six-pack on the table. "Your old man's in the Corps, your mom works at the base, and they didn't teach you manners?" He picks up a bag of charcoal, shakes a pile into a blackened drum cut lengthwise propped atop cinder blocks, douses it with a cup of white gas, and tosses in a match. "You can stay for supper, but I got to work later. I'll drop you off on my way."

The sun-bleached picnic table is as gray and checkered as the trunk of a Joshua tree and Borrego sips a beer as he sits across from the kid watching the flames rise from the pyre of briquettes. Doves coo from their nests in a nearby piñon. Those trapped inside the wire-meshed coop answer mournfully back. The kept quails add their slurred three-note call, *Chi-ca-go, Chi-ca-go.*

"Why don't you let the birds go?" the boy asks. "They're

better off being free."

"Not during hunting season."

The kid hooks a thumb at the desert. "You can't protect them all."

Borrego knows he's right, just as he knows not every rule makes sense, that, like bad decisions made by those with bad information or bad intentions, following them blindly can get you into even worse trouble. "I kept a roadrunner for a while. She had a broken wing. They don't fly much, but they still need their wings. I let her go one morning."

"Because you wanted her to be free?"

"Because I grew tired of catching snakes and spiders for her to eat."

The boy is looking at him now, searching his eyes and face to find his meaning. "How come you know so much about the desert?"

"Because I've always lived in one."

"Always this one?"

"All but a couple years."

"And your parents? Did they work at the base, too?"

Borrego pops opens another beer. Takes a slow sip. Nods.

The boy looks at the trailer. "How long have you lived here?"

Borrego keeps his eyes on the smoke, but sees the image of the roadrunner he holds in his head, sees the iridescent streaks in her beautiful crest, her long tail feathers, her graceful stride when she runs. "'Bout a year or so now."

The kid nods to himself as if confirming something he already knows then asks, "You're not married? You don't have kids?" When Borrego shakes his head, the boy says, "Kinda lonely way out here."

"You sure ask a lot of questions."

He shrugs. "I got a lot of curiosity."

"You'll grow out of it."

The boy pauses, seems to hunker down even further into his oversized sweatshirt, and when he speaks again his voice is softer than before. "Can I ask you another question?" When

Borrego doesn't say no, he says, "What's red mist?"

Borrego runs his forefinger around the top of the can, presses a callous hard against the dull edge of the aluminum opening until it hurts. "Where did you hear that?"

"My neighbor was in his backyard talking to someone, going on about his last tour, what IEDs do to patrols. I heard my dad's name, from over the fence."

"It doesn't mean anything," Borrego says quickly. "Just talk."

He stands and places two hotdogs on the grill even though the coals are still blazing and it's way too hot to cook. He rolls them with a forked stick broken off a coyote willow, trying to keep them from swelling and splitting, the soft brown skin from burning to a cinder. The scarlet flames force him to shut his eyes, but he can still see the red from behind the lids.

After they eat, Borrego tells the kid to get in the Blazer, he'll give him a ride home. But the boy starts talking about how the base is holding maneuvers that night and his mother will be at work until dawn, telling Borrego if he takes him home he'll just slip out the backdoor and try and get as close as he can to the action so he can watch them fire TOWs at junk Caterpillars they set up as targets, see the Apaches strafe a dummy mud compound with their M230s.

"You sure know a lot about the military for a kid," Borrego says.

"It's all my dad ever talks about," the boy says. "I'm going to be a Marine just like him."

Borrego, thinking about the kid's old man, says, "You want, you can come with me, watch while I work."

In the Blazer, Borrego bypasses the main entrance to the park for a sandy wash a couple miles east that leads to an outcropping of boulders the size of haystacks. He tells the boy to wait. Then he follows a jackrabbit path that winds through scrub oak and junipers. It leads to a thick forest of silver cholla, the millions of spines shimmering in the moonlight, their number dwarfed only by the stardust above. Wearing a trenching tool clipped to his web belt, Borrego eases between the clawing limbs to reach the center of the garden where, protected by the bigger silvers, smaller, more exotic night blooming cholla species grow, their flowers open wide. He picks out a Munz's, a snake, a Wiggins', and a beautiful, and begins to dig.

The boy is sitting on the hood of the Blazer when Borrego returns with his prizes. "I didn't hear you coming," the kid says. "You walk so quietly."

"Practice," Borrego says.

"You're not afraid of getting caught stealing?"

"It's only stealing when you take something that belongs to someone else and keep it for yourself. I'm just moving them from one place to another. Some people can hike up here to see them. Others can't leave their patios."

Borrego takes squares of burlap, douses them with a plastic jug of water, rubs them on the ground until they're coated in sand then makes a diaper around the root ball of each cholla, cinching the damp, sandy burlap with hemp twine.

"Will that keep them alive?" the boy asks.

"For the time being."

As he wraps another cholla a dull thud shakes the inky stillness like thunder. A red starburst punches the sky, another follows, and then another.

"Live-fire's started," the boy shouts, and jumps off the hood and begins scrambling up the rocky outcrop. "Best view will be from up there."

"Careful," Borrego calls. "The rock's loose. The scorpions come out at night."

He slams the tailgate shut and goes after him. The outcropping steepens quickly and the surface of the rough granite boulders is coarser than sandpaper and he wishes he'd kept his leather gloves on. The moon shines from behind the highest pinnacle of rock, casting a long shadow toward him as he climbs. He looks up. The boy is standing on top, silhouetted again, his arms outstretched to keep his balance on the tricky footing.

Borrego keeps climbing and when he reaches him, the kid

says, "Look."

From across the wide, downward sloping bajada red and white tracers slash the sky, orange and yellow blooms explode from the ground. Overhead, jets whine unseen and the steady thwap thwap of rotor blades makes Borrego picture a swarm of wasps with their stingers poised.

"Oorah," the boy cheers. "Go get 'em."

The pinnacle they stand on seems to amplify the distant concussions and Borrego has to stick his arms out for balance, too. The rumble coming up through the soles of his boots shakes things loose like an earthquake, only it's not rocks or the walls of houses that begin to fissure and tumble, but those put up around memories. And though he can't see into the darkness, he knows they're out there now, the columns of tanks and APCs and Humvees plowing through dark dunes, trusting the laser trail markers triggered by the advance team of scouts who work alone, out on their own for days dodging enemies, dealing death. The armored column rushes their targets with the fury of a flash flood racing down a bone dry wash as mines explode and wire-guided missiles fired from the backs of black Toyota pickup trucks rain down.

"Cool, huh?" the kid says. "I'll bet you were just like me growing up, sneaking out at night to watch live-fire."

But Borrego doesn't answer as he tries to pick his way carefully through the past three years, as careful as he does now when finding his way back out of a forest of cholla on a moonless night, the trick being to retrace his steps without running into the spines that stuck him on the way in.

After the roar of aircraft dies and the showers from all the tracers fade, Borrego tells the boy it's time to leave and to follow him back down the rocks to the Blazer. But when he reaches it, the kid is nowhere to be seen. He yells, honks the horn, stabs the spotlight into the darkness. When the night grays and the hard rocks turn pink then pale yellow from the first rays of sun, he gives up and leaves the boy behind.

***

Borrego drives straight to La Quinta as the Coachella Valley awakens to the morning light. At Mr. and Mrs. Walker's house a young guy with blond surfer hair and tan legs is skimming leis of purple lantana blossoms from the pool with a long-handle net. "Whoa, brah. You 'bout made me shit sneaking up like that," he says. "Howzit hangin'?" Borrego just nods and goes to work, digging a couple of new holes.

After the pool cleaner leaves, Mrs. Walker pushes open the French doors. She's wearing a white halter top and matching tennis skirt, a thin gold chain gleams around her flat stomach, a crystal flute filled with gold liquid sparkles in her hand.

"*Buenos dias*. How's my cactus garden coming?"

"All done," he says.

"Really? What kind of chollas did you plant for me?"

Borrego shows her.

Like her smile, it's hard to tell when she's frowning. "What's so rare about these? They look like ordinary cactus growing all over." And she waves the crystal flute so hard at the clumps of prickly pear and beavertail crowding the undeveloped lots on the other side of the gates that its contents spill out in a sparkly gold wave.

"No, these are just right for here," Borrego says, gathering his tools.

He can feel her mood shift, as sure as when wind gathers in the heat of the day then careens off the Little San Bernadinos and sweeps back across the Mojave.

"Wait," she says, her voice now a throaty coo. "I still want you to take a look at that bedside lamp in the cabaña. Come on. Let me show it to you."

Borrego knew all along it would come to this, knowing from the other gate-guarded women it would only be the one time, Mrs. Walker needing to tell herself afterward that it was because he was so special, a shaman when it came to creating desert landscapes, not just some once-a-week guy with a gas-powered leaf blower strapped to his back.

"Sorry," he says, heading toward the Blazer parked out front. "I got some other place I got to be."

***

It's not that dark inside and the air conditioner rattles and hums against the sun beating down on the flat roof of a squat building made of cinderblocks and painted ochre. The bartender's buzz cut is as mottled as a chunk of snowflake obsidian and his arching brows and squared moustache are more white than black. He pulls a draft of Bud Lite and slides the glass in front of Borrego.

"You sure you don't want a margarita? Friday's margarita night here at the Post."

"Beer's fine," Borrego says.

"You gonna stay for the dinner? Friday's taco night. They'll be serving it up another hour or so."

Borrego shakes his head. "Just the beer."

He looks around the room. The linoleum floors are yellowed and four old guys are playing gin rummy at a nearby table. All wear slouch caps festooned with sew-on VFW Post numbers and metal campaign pins. Framed displays of service emblems and company badges crowd the paneled walls. The colors hang on oak staffs floor-mounted in the corner.

The bartender says, "So, when will you start?"

Borrego skates the glass around the polished surface of the mahogany bar. "Maybe day after tomorrow. There's something I got to do first."

"Well, the members'll appreciate your offer, that's a fact. Front of the place needs some spit and polish. When the wind blows, them dead palm fronds make so much racket the old dogs over there complain they got to turn their hearing aids down."

The bartender's face is all cracks and crevices that widen as he grins. He showers a dirty glass under the faucet. "You know you didn't have to offer to work for free to be welcome in here. You earned the right same as them." He nods at the card players.

Borrego just pushes away his now-empty glass, reaches into his back pocket for his wallet. "How much I owe you for the beer?"

The bartender puts the glass he's been washing on a plastic

four horses and he hauled the sun across the sky. Every day."

The girl brightened. She tilted her face and held her hands in front of her like she was gripping reins. "What color of horses?"

He could hear the way his ma used to read it at bedtime before she started drinking so much. "White. And they had wings, too."

"Do you have a horse?"

She looked disappointed when he said no and as soon as he said it he wished he could take it back.

She stamped her tennis shoe-hoof. "So why are you called Apollo if you don't even have a horse?"

He was trying to think fast now, clutching the comic book as the words came tumbling, stumbling out. "Because all the neat stuff he does. He takes care of things and always tells the truth no matter what. He can see into the future, too. Ma said if I could see good luck coming or get out of the way if it was bad it'd make her job a whole lot easier."

"Can you?"

Polly looked down at the marks she'd pawed in the sand, not wanting to say no to her again, thinking how he sure didn't see it coming a year before when he took the Chrysler New Yorker the man who came home with his ma had parked in front of the trailer. He'd called Polly a big mama's boy and tossed him the keys and told him to go sit in the car and play the radio while his ma and him had a drink. "And don't play with yourself while you're at it," the man had hollered. When the cops pulled him over, they wouldn't listen to him when he explained the reason he'd driven off in it was because he could still hear the man laughing at him when he was sitting out front even with the radio turned on full blast.

"Are you from Barstow?" he asked.

The girl tossed her ponytail. "We're only living here for a little while. Poppa got a job driving a truck. As soon as school starts we're going to move into a big house with a swimming pool and get a puppy."

Polly frowned. "Well, I'm going move, too. Just as soon as

I save enough to buy a car. I make lots a money bagging."

A short man who'd rolled the bottom of his sleeveless undershirt up over his belly marched across the courtyard.

"What did I tell you, girl? Get back to the room. Quick, now." His nostrils flared as he spoke. His voice sounded like one of the semi-trucks downshifting on the four-lane out front.

"This is Polly, Poppa," Lilibeth said, her voice younger, quieter. "We were just talking. Nothing else."

"I don't care what the big dumbshit's name is. He got no business talking to you. Now get home." The man's face had turned the color of the top of his left arm. Grains of sand misted the black hairs growing from his shoulders.

The girl bowed, her ponytail hanging limp down her narrow back. She shuffled away.

The man in the undershirt turned on Polly. "What the fuck you looking at?" His breath smelled of old hamburgers.

Polly held the comic book tight to his stomach. "Nothing."

"I catch you sniffing around my daughters again, I'll kick a jack handle so far up your ass you'll need a tire iron to eat, you read me?"

"Uh, huh."

"What's that?"

"Uh, yes, sir."

"Where your parents at?"

"They're gone."

"They get back, I'm gonna have words with 'em. Tell 'em they can't teach you to keep your pecker zipped, I sure as hell will. You read me?"

"Uh, huh. I mean, yes, sir."

The man spit, the dark globules plopping between Polly's feet, separating in the sand like amoebas, sending him scuttling backwards. He retreated into his unit and put the door chain on before going to bed that night.

***

The shadows disappear as the goats move down pasture. The old man turns away from the clothesline to start in on the next chore. It's important to do them in order so as not to forget one. The rules of the program are clear. There's no room for a mess-up. None. The couple can always send him back to Susanville early. They can send him back for good, they want, and not pick him up on Monday morning. He remembers what it was like with no work release program to look forward to, what it was like his very first year inside Corcoran when the wolves cornered him in the laundry room.

The old man heads for the barn. A half dozen brown hens scratch for seed in the yard beside it, their yellow beaks and feet in constant motion as they dance. One step forward, two steps back. He pushes open the double-wide doors and hesitates before stepping into the half-light, straining to see if wolves are waiting in the shadows, listening for a tell-tale: an eager pant, a muscle flexing against denim, the swish of a shiv.

His eyes adjust and he spots the pile of fat feed bags the delivery truck had dumped that morning. The old man stoops and lifts the top one, hugs the soft bag to his chest like it's a pudgy child, waddling as he carries it to a horse stall now used to store feed. By the time he finishes moving all the bags and making neat stacks, rivulets of sweat are running down his back, dampening the inside of his jumpsuit. He's breathing hard and catches a scent still lingering in the stall that makes him drop to his knees in the straw and close his eyes and picture horses running free of bridle and bit.

***

Of all the cereals, Polly liked Rice Krispies best. Snap. Crackle. Pop. He was leaning over a bowl to listen for his favorite character when an idling big rig rattled his kitchenette window. He peeked out the checkered curtains to see Lilibeth's father with one foot on the running board.

"I'm on the fuckin' road all week long," he was yelling at her mother. "Don't let them two girls out of your sight. You read me?"

Lilibeth's mother didn't come outside much and when she did she always wore dark glasses and stared at the ground. She handed him a dirty red gym bag without looking up.

Polly hurried home from work that afternoon. He'd bought

some special treats using his bagger's discount. After he put them away he went out and sat on his front stoop. He didn't have to wait long before the girls galloped by.

Polly wiped his brow. "Sure is hot, hot enough to fry an egg."

Lilibeth neighed and pulled to a stop. With her little sister nickering beside her, she said, "Poppa says we're going to have a pool when we move. We'll be able to cool off whenever we want."

"I got something cool you off right now, you want."

"What is it?"

"It's my own special invention. I call it a Nut Float."

"A what?"

"Come on inside and I'll show you." He stood up and gestured toward the door to his unit.

Lilibeth backed up skittishly, reining in her sister as she did. "We can't. Poppa said."

Polly waved his hands. "Okay, okay. I'll bring everything out here. Just you wait." He hurried inside and retrieved the quart of 7 UP and carton of Rocky Road from the ice box. "See," he said, sitting back on the front stoop and filling a plastic tumbler half way to the top with the bubbly liquid, then spooning in a big dollop of ice cream. "The nuts and marshmallows all float to the top. It tastes really good. Here, try it." He made another and handed it to her little sister.

The girls finished them, grinning beneath chocolate moustaches. Then they started galloping around the courtyard, whinnying with delight.

All that week Polly couldn't wait for work to end. He brought something home each time. Candy, comic books, Cracker Jacks. One afternoon while he was bagging, Jeannie, the check-out clerk, sent him to exchange a dented can. Passing through the sundries aisle he couldn't believe his eyes. A white plastic horse stood on the same shelf that held the bags of jacks, rubber balls, and blowing bubbles soap.

He gave it to Lilibeth as soon as he got back. "If it had wings, it'd be just like the ones pulling the chariot."

"Why, it's the most beautiful thing I've ever seen." She held it straight out at her side and raced it around the courtyard, her little sister chasing right behind.

As he was getting ready for bed that night someone pounded on his door. Before he could turn the knob the door crashed open, breaking the chain, its edge catching the side of his head, knocking him backward. Lilibeth's father grabbed him by his pajama top and jerked him forward. The man's eyes blazed. He spit when he talked.

"You fat fuck, I told you to keep away. You think I don't know what you're up to?"

Polly tasted the blood before he felt the fist smash into his jaw. As he tried to cover his head, more blows slammed into him. Bright lights exploded in the darkened room. Lilibeth's father punched him two, three, four more times. Polly lost count. His ears rang then all went silent. When the sound came rushing back, he lay curled in a ball. The man loomed over him, snapping the legs off the plastic horse and flinging them at him.

"Next time it'll be your fuckin' arms and legs," he roared. "I'll fuckin' tear 'em off, so help me God, I will." He hurled the limbless torso at him and stomped out.

Polly almost blacked out again when he tried to sit up. It took forever to stand. He lurched into the bathroom and pulled the light chain. He had to stoop to look into the mirror hanging over the rusty sink. His face was two times too big, his eye nearly swollen shut. What would the store manager think when he got to work? What would County do if he got fired?

Trying to think, Polly pictured himself holding a dishtowel wrapped around ice cubes against his ma's forehead every morning, heard her saying what she always said, that Apollo the god had the healing touch. He picked up the plastic trash can next to the toilet and staggered over to the front window. No lights yellowed any of the other units' windows. He tucked the trash can under his arm, eased open the door and checked the path to the ice machine where he planned to fill up the can. As he started toward it a big rig roared down the four-lane out front, sucking the air from the courtyard as it passed. The backdraft tugged at all the checkered curtains hanging in front of all the open windows, making them snap like laundry fluttering in the wind. Terrified he'd be caught out in the open, Polly glanced at Lilibeth's unit. He could see straight into the kitchenette. The girl was looking right back at him, her eyes shiny with tears. She was sprawled across the top of the blue Formica table, her chest pushed flat against it. Her father, wearing only a sleeveless undershirt, was straddling her, holding the hem of her nightgown up with one hand, yanking her ponytail with the other as he bucked up and down.

***

The old man leaves the darkened barn for daylight. He carries a pair of bullnose pliers and a stretcher bar down to the wire perimeter fence to check for loose strands. When he gets there he finds a kid tangled in the mesh. It bleats and thrashes but the nannies and billies pay it no mind. The old man locks his arm around the kid's neck and tenderly pulls its front hoofs free. When he lets it go the young goat springs away and returns to the herd, never looking back.

Dusting his hands, the old man begins walking along the fenceline, plucking the wire horizontals and stays as he goes. Most resist, but some twang. These he cinches up tight with the tools. As he works, he pictures another fence, a high one with coils of barbwire on the top, a fenced yard where a boy walks in circles by himself hoping he's invisible to wolves like 400-pound Frankie who does the holding in the laundry room while Ortiz does the cutting, Ortiz's pocked face the color of a handful of Sugar Babies as he explains he's got daughters of his own on the outside to protect against short eyes and be thankful it's only his balls and not his throat.

The wind picks up, making the woven wire mesh whistle and whine. Despite the sun, the cries chill him, and the old man hears those of others and those of his own, the cries he could stifle and those he could not. There were cries of young boys and cries of grown men. And, loudest of all, cries that could not and never would be heard at all.

***

Polly was stocking shelves, able to reach the top without need of a step-ladder, carefully lining up the cans of peaches and fruit cocktail so their labels faced right-side out. Lilibeth and her little sister walked in and stood at the end of the aisle. He hadn't spoken to them in weeks, avoiding everyone living at the motor court by working double shifts and weekends. Lilibeth told the younger girl to wait for her then walked over. She took a can of peaches from the cardboard box on the floor and handed it to him.

Too embarrassed to look at her, he kept his eyes on the shelf as he placed the can. "Thanks," he mumbled.

"Momma sent my sister and me to do the shopping," she said. "She's sick in bed."

He searched the aisle, afraid her father would show up any minute. "Where's your pa at?"

"Poppa's away at work." She handed him another can of peaches. "How come you don't sit out on your stoop anymore?"

"They need me here bagging. I got an important job, you know."

When she didn't say anything, he said, "How come you ask?"

Lilibeth stared down at the box of canned peaches. "I don't know. Just wondered why my little sister and me haven't seen you around is all." She paused. "You're not mad or anything, are you?"

Polly glanced at the smaller girl. She was twirling around and around singing to herself, gazing up at the ceiling, her ponytail not quite as long as Lilibeth's. He wished he had a sister like Apollo had. They were twins and did everything together, like hunted with bows and arrows. One of his ma's favorite stories was how Apollo and Artemis protected their ma when another goddess was mean to her. That's what they did, looked out for her, took care of each other, too.

He wished he was as brave as Apollo. It made him feel bad that he didn't do anything the night he saw into Lilibeth's kitchenette. He thought about Lilibeth's father, the way he kept hitting him, making him more scared than he'd ever been at Chino Boys, making him feel more alone than when he was called into the warden's office and told his ma had died. Thinking about it, thinking about Lilibeth's father now, he tightened his grip on the can of peaches, so tight he felt like he could squeeze the sides together, squeeze the syrupy slices of cling peaches right through the tin top until they spilled out and slopped onto the grocery store's linoleum floor and wiggled away like goldfish. He kept thinking, thinking hard.

"You got to tell someone," he finally said. "You got to tell your ma."

Lilibeth looked up, paling, so pale her freckles all but disappeared. "You don't understand." She started fighting tears.

"Well, somebody should tell somebody something."

She put her hand up quickly, holding her palm toward him, her words tumbling out. "No. You got to promise you won't tell anyone. I'll be in big trouble and get punished like before. I don't want my little sister to get punished, ever. You can't say a word. Ever. Not a word. Never tell no one. Just don't speak about it. At all. Please? Pretty please? Promise you won't ever say a word, cross your heart and hope to die."

He crossed his heart with the can of peaches, but he hadn't meant himself as the somebody who should tell somebody. Who would he tell? Jeannie? The store manager? The man at County who dropped him off at the motor court and warned him to stay out of trouble? The police? He remembered the way they treated him when they caught him in the big Chrysler New Yorker with all its shiny chrome, how they didn't believe him when he told them the man had given him the keys, how they took the man's word over his when the man said he didn't know him or know his ma, either, said Polly was just a low-down punk car thief. He remembered how the police had laughed at him just like the man with the Chrysler had when Polly told them they had to believe him because he was just like the Greek god, that he could only tell the truth, no matter

animals are conditioned by the routine and don't balk or attempt to flee. In the pens, he checks to make sure there is sufficient water and feed in the troughs to last the night, clean straw in the beds. Some of the nannies are already bending their knees and then their hocks to lie down and chew their cuds. He likes hearing that, the sound wet and rhythmic like soft rain dripping slowly from eaves.

A couple of billies start sparring, butting their heads and rearing on hind legs as they punch with their front hoofs. The old man loops braided ropes over their heads and tethers them to stakes at opposite ends of the pen. He doesn't like to confine them, but sometimes there's no choice and it's for their own good to keep them from getting hurt, like doing something to get put in solitary on purpose in order to stay out of the reach of wolves, no matter how afraid it makes you, how many years it adds to being inside.

The old man turns his eyes from the tethered billies who strain against their ropes like a wolf caught alone trying to break free from big hands around his neck that turn his caramel candy face blue. He watches as the nannies and their kids snuggle down in their beds of straw and tells himself it's always better to be safe than sorry for what you've done.

***

Polly sat on his bed in the dark and waited, hugging the plastic trash can filled with the contents of the ice box – two bottles of 7 UP, a half carton of milk and a package of Oscar Mayer bologna. Seven slices were left in the loaf of Wonder Bread. He packed that, too, along with Rice Krispies, bowls and spoons. He was trying to remember the story about when Apollo got mad that his sister was always going hunting with the giant Orion so he challenged her to an archery contest and tricked her into shooting an arrow at a target way out at sea but it was really Orion's head, how mad Artemis got when she found out he'd tricked her. Tricking wasn't the same as not telling the truth. Polly almost didn't hear the door push open.

Lilibeth was clutching her little sister's hand. The younger girl's face was puffy with sleep. "Where's your new car?" she asked.

"Down the street. Are you sure you didn't wake your ma?"

Lilibeth shook her head. "I told you, she's sick in bed. She takes medicine and sleeps 'til after lunch. We'll be back by then, right?"

He nodded. "And your pa's still gone?"

"Uh, huh."

"Okay. I'm going go get the car now. You count to a hundred then walk straight out front. I'll pick you up there. You got to be quiet, remember?"

Polly carried the plastic trash can packed with food and hurried down the four-lane to a used car lot he passed on the way to the grocery store every day. He already knew which one he was going to take, a white four-door Impala. He pulled a screwdriver he used for prying apart packing crates from his back pocket and jammed it into the driver's side door lock. He gave it a powerful twist and the knob popped up. It sounded as loud as a rifle shot. He had the door opened and closed as fast as he could, hoping no one saw the dome light blink on and off. He reached under the dash, crossed the wires like he remembered hearing how at Chino Boys and, when the engine caught, felt the feeling he got when he drove off in the big Chrysler New Yorker.

Lilibeth had her arm around her little sister's shoulders as he eased up to the motor court's entrance. He leaned across the wide front seat and opened the door. "Don't slam it," he whispered.

As the lights of Barstow retreated in the rearview mirror, Polly stepped on the gas and pictured a chariot racing across the sky, everyone depending on it to pull the sun each day. He looked over at the two girls sitting beside him, the dim glow of the dashboard lights making their faces shine. It made him feel good.

"Wild horses, here we come," he said.

"How much longer?" Lilibeth said.

"Not too much." Polly concentrated on the headlights, running the route over in his mind that Jeannie had traced with her red polished fingernail on a folded roadmap at her check-out station after he asked her where the Indian reservation was. They sped through a flat stretch of desert, the only relief an occasional road sign peppered by shotgun blasts and rifle shot.

"Now that you bought your car, are you going to move like you said?" Lilibeth asked.

"Uh, maybe. I don't know yet. When are you going to move into a big house with a pool and get a puppy?"

Lilibeth was quiet for a few moments. "I don't care about a pool anymore. Or a puppy." She tightened her arm around her little sister. "She won't want a puppy, either."

"Oh," Polly said, thinking that maybe he'd stay, too. He liked bagging. He liked stocking the shelves. Maybe after a while they'd move him up. Maybe to check-out clerk. They wore white shirts and ties.

Lilibeth started to shiver. "I don't feel so good."

"Wait til you see the wild horses," he said. "They'll make you feel better."

They drove in silence. Once or twice Polly caught himself drifting off. He gripped the steering wheel tighter and opened the wing window, directing the dark flow of air right into his face. It smelled of sage. The four-lane narrowed into a two-lane. He followed the sign at the intersection. In several miles the road turned to gravel. It was bumpy and the going slow. Eventually the road became dirt. He spotted a turnout and, figuring it was as good as any, pulled off and stopped the engine.

Lilibeth and her sister huddled together against the passenger door and appeared to be asleep. Polly made sure the dome light was off before opening the door. The air outside lay still and the stars were melting into dawn. He walked behind the car's rear bumper to urinate. A coyote yipped in the distance as he unzipped his fly. Startled, he strained to see through the pale light. Shaggy giants with outstretched arms surrounded him. His penis shriveled in his hand. He looked closer at the approaching monsters. They were Joshua trees. When he got back to the car Lilibeth was awake.

"Do you want some Rice Krispies?" he asked.

"Okay."

"Is your little sister awake?"

She shook her head. "Are we there yet? Where are the horses?"

"They'll be along any time now." He poured her a bowl of cereal and handed it to her.

Lilibeth shivered again. Her forehead started to glisten. She began rocking and moaned.

"What's the matter?" Polly said.

"I don't feel so good."

"Maybe the milk's gone sour. I get the ones they're going throw out. They don't cost nothing."

She leaned forward and threw up. The vomit splashed into her lap, sprayed the dashboard.

Polly scrambled out of the car and helped her out, standing beside her as she threw up again. When she finished, he peeled off his shirt and wiped her face with it. He rubbed the front of her clothes with it, too, but her blouse was soaked.

"You should take that off and put my jacket on." He got it from the back seat and handed it to her.

Polly opened a bottle of 7 UP and poured some on the car seat and dash, wiping them with his shirt, careful not to wake the younger girl. Then he walked to the edge of the turnout and kept his back to Lilibeth while she changed. Just beyond the turnout was a pond, the still water the color of lead. Beyond spread a rocky flat plain spotted with sagebrush, saltbush and clumps of dried prairie clover. The hump of a mesa rose on the horizon. The wild horses come here for the water, he told himself.

When Lilibeth had finished changing, he carried her blouse and his dirty shirt down to the pond. Its shore was crusty and white and smelled like salt. Dead trees stuck out of the shallows, naked of leaves, the bark bleached white as bone. A pair of vultures hunched on a limb, bigger than crows and just as black but with no feathers on their heads. They watched him as he knelt and plunged the dirty clothes into the water, the bits of vomit floating up and bobbing on the metallic surface. Polly picked up a rock to throw at the birds, but decided against it. They hadn't done anything to him. He fished the blouse and shirt out of the water and scrambled back to the white Chevy. Lilibeth was wrapped in his jacket now, her eyes closed, her head resting on her little sister's shoulder. He spread the wet clothes on the Impala's long hood to dry. He scanned the plain between the pond and mesa and hoped for horses. Feeling cold without his shirt on, he climbed into the sedan's back seat and stretched out, hugging himself, resting his head on the plastic trash can, trying to remember the story about when Apollo let his son drive the chariot, but the boy wasn't strong enough and flew so low the Earth burst into flames and Zeus got so mad he threw a thunderbolt right through the boy's heart. He closed his eyes.

White horses reared then charged, sparks shooting from their hoofs. The chariot took off and he had to grip the reins tight. Everything was ablaze in hot golden light as they streaked across the sky, too low and too fast, he knew, but there was no slowing them down now. The horses snorted and thundered as they galloped, their wings making deep whooping sounds as they beat. Shadows caught his eye and he looked up to see a pair of giant vultures as black as coal chasing them, their featherless heads as orange as cling peaches, their beaks agape, their outstretched talons reaching for him. Faster, he commanded the horses, faster. But the shrieks of the birds were just as loud.

The noise pulled him from the dream, but the sound was coming from the front seat. "Please, don't," Lilibeth cried. "Please, don't."

Before Polly had time to sit up the backdoors ripped open and fingers as hard as iron grabbed his wrists and ankles and yanked him in opposite direction. He started kicking and twisting to get free. The plastic trash can slid off the seat, spilled milk and 7 UP puddling together on the car floor. The hands gripping him tightened and pulled harder, stretching him even more. Both shoulders popped and Polly saw a white flame as the pain burned through him like a hurled thunderbolt. Still, he kept thrashing.

Lilibeth cried out again. Polly twisted toward her voice. She was staring over the back of the front seat at him, pleading, "Please, don't," and he knew what she meant and if he could've crossed his heart he would've. Then she pushed her little sister out of the car, grabbed her by the hand and started to run. Polly twisted again so he could see past the uniformed man with the holster gripping his ankles. The two girls galloped down the dirt road, their ponytails streaming behind, dust kicking up from their tennis shoe hoofs.

"Look, he stripped the one and dressed her in his own clothes. Fucking pervert. No wonder why they're running from him the first chance they get." The cop gripping Polly's wrists gave a vicious twist.

"Should I go get them?" the other cop asked.

"Help me cuff him first. He's a big fucker, isn't he?"

They wrestled him out of the Chevy. The cop yanking his arms behind him leaned in close. "You should thank us for finding you before those little girls' daddy did. He'd've killed you on the spot for what you done to them." He put the handcuffs on, clicking them tight. "Give it up, buddy boy. Better to spill your guts now and save everybody a whole lot of trouble later."

Polly looked back to where the girls had run, to the rocky plain and the mesa beyond. A cloud of dust was rising now, he was sure of it, kicked up by a herd of wild horses galloping fast and free.

The cop leaned in close again. "What's the matter? Cat got your tongue?"

Polly kept his eyes straight ahead, remembering he'd crossed his heart and hoped to die, remembering what his ma always said, to be like Apollo and if you can't tell the truth, then don't say nothing at all. Ever again. Not ever.

"Suit yourself," the cop said. "We got you dead to rights anyway. They're going to lock you up and throw away the key."

But Polly didn't hear him. He was too busying listening for

the whinny of wild horses in the wind.

***

The old man returns to the clothesline to complete the last job of the day. It's also his last for the week. In the morning the Muellers will take him back to Susanville like they do every Saturday. He puts his hands to the rope where the sheets hang as if to steady himself, but instead grips it like reins and watches the sun race toward the horizon, seeing in the final rays the white flash of four flying horses. The bed linens are dry now, the dampness gone without wringing, the wrinkles carried away by the high desert wind. He unclips the clothespins from the first sheet and folds it lengthwise where he stands, old and hunched but still big enough to keep the ends from being sullied by the ground. The creases sharp, the corners lined up just right, he smoothes the crisp fabric with strong fingers whose grip can't be broken as he tucks and folds. Then, before placing it in the basket, the old man presses the clean folded square against his cheek, nuzzling the warmth of the sun still trapped in its cotton weave, wishing he could hold onto it to help make the nights he spends on the inside waiting for Monday morning not seem so dark.

SALT

The sun hasn't turned the gray water green and the sea lions are still hunkered in their haul-outs. The tide chases the moon as a salmon boat wallows in its berth in a small harbor on the North Coast, its hold slopping with bilge. The corners of a loose tarp flap. Rigging bangs against the wheelhouse. Bottles roll beside the metal bunk, reminders that no matter how much Wes drinks he'll never drown the taste of salt.

It's more than thirst and the shakes and the need for a smoke and another oxy that drives him to throw off the dank sheets. Wes rubs a jaw itching from weeks of a blade left to rust on the galley sink, pulls on his gumboots, and staggers outside and up the slanted dock. The sky lightens as he reaches his pickup, the faded blue cab now rimed with seagull shit. The engine cranks once, twice, three times, then fires.

Wes straddles the center line of the narrow two-lane blacktop that follows the river from its mouth to its source high in the mountains. His stomach aches, his head pounds, his skin flashes hot and cold as he steers up the winding climb. When a logging truck comes at him around a blind curve he is trying not to picture the child-proof plastic pill bottle back on the boat. The trucker hits his horn, forcing Wes to yank the wheel and skid to a stop on the shoulder. The double-trailer kicks up gravel as it thunders by, passing so close he can see where the come-alongs that bind the limbless redwoods have bit deep into their bark, leaving the cambium raw and exposed, the color of flesh spent too long in water.

He tries to blink away the image and reaches above the visor for a crumpled pack of Basics. It takes both hands to mate the wavering tip to the glowing orange coil of the pickup's lighter. The tobacco is stale and the acrid pall can't hide the truth: he still tastes salt.

A few miles short of the summit the canyon swallows the river. Wes follows a gravel road leading down into it, but the going is slow as it winds through a thickening forest. Gravel turns into dirt, dirt into mud. Two ruts turn into one. He parks and continues on foot. An owl hoots as he hikes down a series of steep switchbacks, mud squishing beneath boot soles made for pitching decks, not slippery mountainsides. The moist, feral scent of rotting wood fills his nostrils. Raindrops collect at the tips of waxy needles; they grow to the size of pearls before gravity wins out. A spoor from a banana slug shimmers on the path like a discarded snakeskin. Reefs of ledge fungi whiten the sides of downed logs. Unseen things rustle the understory and furtive shadows scurry away. He remembers his grandpa telling him that when he was a boy there were still grizzlies to hunt. He tries to recall the last report of a mountain lion attack in Humboldt County and pictures his son, Benny, sitting at the kitchen table doing his homework, reading a schoolbook with drawings of the saber tooth cats that prowled California 10,000 years before.

The trail grows steeper, fainter, slicker. The forest grows thicker, darker. It feels as if he's entered a place where all the rules of nature have been suspended, where the laws that govern predators to still their instinct for violence against their own kind have been silenced. He is far from what he knows, far from what he's looking for, tired, pissed-off, with his shipwreck-damaged back hurting more than ever, Wes drops to his knees and tucks his fists into his armpits, knowing he is lost.

Wind blows through the redwoods sending the thick limbs sawing against each other like cricket forewings, chirring and lowing. He imagines himself climbing to the top of the tallest. Up there, he knows, the sun will be shining bright and he'll be able to see his destination. He'll be able to hold his face to the yellow beam, bask in its warmth, remember the sunny afternoons when they used to spread a picnic blanket atop the tall grass that waved on the bluffs above the harbor, see Maggie and his parents and his grandpa sitting on it, eating *lefse* and *fatigman*, Benny there, too, his eyes sparkling, his head nodding to the throb and pulse of hip-hop pounding through his earbuds, his orange wool watch cap pulled low, the cap Maggie had knitted for him, saying he needed it to keep warm on the boat though Wes knows she chose the color as a beacon so he can always keep an eye on Benny from the wheelhouse as the boy scrambles around the deck, ducking under the troll outriggers, baiting hooks, clipping on dodgers and hoochies, reeling in lines.

Wes wishes he could be there on the picnic blanket with them right now, holding his wife close, watching his son play, listening to his dad and grandpa swap lies about fishing while they sneak sips of vodka – what his grandpa calls Viking tears – from plastic cups, his mother insisting that everyone eat more but be sure to save room for Cloudberry Cream and Bergen rum balls. But he knows he cannot, so he gets up and follows the wind as it blows up the steep canyon, down to the river and the freshwater to wash away the taste of salt.

At the river, the air is filled with the buzz of insects. Clouds of mayflies billow. Water dancers propel themselves across a long, languid pool by pushing up and down on their own reflections, as if making love to a mirror. The pool is fed by a series of falls that cascade over granite boulders glinting with quartz. Wes knows salmon are holding there, gathering strength before making the jump to reach their spawning grounds above. With his hand, he shades his eyes as he searches the pool. Sure enough, thick, long silhouettes of king salmon darken the water.

The first time his father had brought him here to see salmon spawning Wes was seven years old. They had followed a shallow stream off the main fork where the humped backs of the fish stuck out of the water like smooth river rocks. When a female swept her tail back and forth in a bed of gravel covered by no more than a couple inches of clear, cold water, his father explained what was old as life itself.

"See, she's digging a nest," Leif said, "only it's not called a nest but a redd, like the color only with two d's. Now she's laying her eggs."

The fish deposited a clump that looked like the huckleberries Wes's mother picked to make jam. When she finished, a male darted in and hunkered over the redd, his powerful crooked jaws agape, his heaving silvery sides aflame with red streaks. The water turned milky.

"Well, there you go, sure," Leif said, brushing his hands back and forth as if dusting them off.

And Wes had asked what came next.

Leif scowled. "Well, they die, of course. Their job's over, sure. They'll be dead in a week. If they don't wash up on the bank, they'll rot in the river. Keeps it healthy like."

Wes said it didn't make sense. All that work dodging hooks and nets? Fighting the falls to come up river? Their babies, they never get to see them grow up?

"They're just fish," his father replied. "It's the way it is. The smolts, they grow up and do the same. But not every smolt reaches the sea."

Wes asked why they would willingly return to the place of their birth that would surely be the place of their death, but Leif rolled his neck like trying to loosen a knot in his powerful shoulders. "Now that's enough damn fool questions," he said, jutting his bearded chin, making Wes picture Cape Mendocino silhouetted between sea and sky. "Come on. We gotta get going, sure, if we're going to get going."

Wes crouches and cups his hands and dips them into the river and brings the water to his lips. Drinking, he thinks about all the years he'd spent catching salmon with his dad and grandpa and then his own son, and all that had happened on a day that would always be yesterday no matter how many years pass by, and he wonders if he's learned anything at all.

The water is cold, quenching, but still he can taste the salt that seared his throat the day the boat rolled over and he dove again and again to try and save Benny.

***

Wes spends the next two weeks righting the boat. He pumps the bilge, scrubs the decks, and scrapes the hull's waterline. When it is finally shipshape, when the troll reels are all re-rigged with new airplane cable and monofilament line and the big Detroit diesel below deck hums without a cough, he washes and shaves, tucks a fresh shirt into his jeans, and returns to his home on the bluff with the view of the sea.

Climbing the stairs to the second floor feels like stepping from the wheelhouse onto the bow just as it noses into a trough and a wave slams over the railing. Wes has to reach for the banister to steady himself. Maggie is sitting on Benny's bed, staring out the window, and he takes a deep breath before entering the room. No dust spots the furniture, no mothballs sour the air. The laptop on the desk is open, three tiny blue lights blinking on the keyboard. A clean sweatshirt hangs over the back of the chair. The books and CDs on the shelves are straight. All the posters of the hip- hop artists are firmly tacked at the corners, the calendar hanging on the corkboard flipped to the current month.

"Hey," he says. "You cut your hair. It looks good."

When she doesn't answer, he sits beside her and follows her gaze toward the window. Their framed reflection stares back from the pane, their faces slightly out of focus, bathed in sepia tones like an old-time photograph, turning her red hair auburn, washing out her freckles. Wes wants to put his hand on hers, but doesn't.

"I'd give anything," he starts. The words catch so he tries again. "You know I'd have traded places with him if I could. I would've given my life without blinking an eye."

Maggie stiffens. "Do you think you're the only one? You

think I wouldn't have?"

"But it was me on the boat. I'm the skipper. He was my responsibility."

Her cheeks redden. "Don't you dare try and take that away from me. I have the right to blame myself, too."

It's like he's back under the water again, floundering around to find him, not knowing which way is up or down, hoping above hope that the bright orange cap will guide him through the darkness. "I don't want you to hurt anymore," he says.

"I'd rather feel pain than nothing at all. Pills? Vodka? It'd be like he'd never lived."

Wes wants to say that it's all because of the ruptured disks from when the big wave had struck and rolled them upside down, but he sucks his teeth instead. When the silence gets too much, he says, "I'm in uncharted waters here. You want me to say I fucked up? Okay. I fucked up. Big time."

She doesn't answer.

"Come on. Just tell me what you want."

Maggie's reflection pales. Her words are barely a whisper. "What you can't give me. What no one can. Not ever again."

"I would if I could."

"But you can't."

He has no answer to that.

She shifts on the mattress. "We can't pretend it didn't happen. Everything's different now." She clutches her hands on her lap. "I trusted you."

"I know you did, and I always tried to keep him safe." Wes thinks about how he'd made the boy wear gumboots two sizes too big so they'd be easier to kick off, the cap the color of a beacon. "I tried to save him. I did. But no matter how hard I tried, I just couldn't reach him."

She sighs. "You still don't get it. I'm not talking about then. I'm talking about now."

He feels everything slipping away again. "You're right. I don't get a fucking thing."

Maggie's sigh is louder this time. Wes looks at the window. Sunlight is hitting it, dissolving both their reflections, turning the glass clear. He can see the yard, Benny's dog nosing around the blue-bloomed ceanothus bushes looking for something that can never be found. He stares at the ocean beyond. It's a scene he's seen a million times, but now it's like he's never seen it before. Maggie looks different, too. Lines scar her face and the laughter is missing from her emerald eyes. It feels like it was two other people who used to lay in bed after making love and the man would braid a hank of the woman's fiery hair and loop it over his thumb and say, "Look. It's a hawser." And she would say, "I guess that makes us really mooried." And they'd laugh and make love again.

He stands. "I got to go. They reopened the salmon season, but no one knows for how long. When I get back, well, maybe we can try and sort things out. See where we stand."

Wes waits, hoping Maggie will say what she used to always say whenever he put out to sea. "Catch your limit," she'd say. And he'd always say right back, "I already did." He keeps listening for it as he heads out the door, but all he hears are the creak of the floorboards and the shudder of the windowpanes.

***

A week later, Wes is anchored for the night in the lee of Point Delgado. The moon is full, spilling a milky trail that wavers on the gently rolling water. He stands on the aft deck, leaning against the transom, smoking a cigarette and nursing a coffee mug filled with Viking tears. It's quiet but for the lapping against the hull and the soft scrub of wavelets washing onto the black sand beach behind. Watching the cold points of starlight in the sky, he thinks about what he knows and what he doesn't.

He knows how to fish. He knows how to fix a boat. He knows that in the sound of a wave is the echo of every wave that has ever broke, that they are the language of life, untranslatable words that tell the story of the planet's beginning when water covered all, when the molten core of the earth exploded beneath the seas and rose to the surface like an emergent insect in search of light and oxygen, when a singular continent broke into pieces and began to drift, when the first creatures crawled ashore from the primordial ooze, when birds evolved from dinosaurs and mammals first walked.

He knows that he is really no different than the salmon he fishes for. The first time he and Maggie had made love they were both seventeen. After he entered her and they were locked in embrace and had found their rhythm and were racing toward climax, he pictured a great school of silvery fish slicing through water, their fins tucked tight against their muscular torpedo bodies, bubbles trailing behind like specks trapped inside polished aquamarine, the gash of their gills as bright as fresh blood, their eyes fixed on a destination that had been seared into their brains at birth, unforgotten during the years they traveled the ocean wide. A school of thousands, they moved as one, speeding in unison, a singular cell pulsing through the watery universe like stardust gathered by gravity and bound by speed burning across a night sky. The school stopped for nothing, never scattering. Nothing could halt their shared purpose, nothing could make them falter. And as Maggie tightened her arms and legs around him, he saw the salmon speed on and on, coursing around a forested headland and straight into the mouth of a river from their long ago past, now suddenly familiar. Up, up the freshwater's length the school surged until, finally, reaching the banks of their beginning, the silvery mass exploded into a whirling cloud streaked red with roe.

Wes knows that clouds form over the sea and break on mountaintops. The rain washes over the rocks as it gathers and runs to where it came. The surf tumbles everything together and the ocean decides what to keep and what to give back. Beaches come and go with the tide. Dunes rise and fall, and driftwood as big and bleached as whale bones gets picked clean in the night, erased like footsteps in the wind and the call of shorebirds already flown by. The river will always take its water from the sea just as the sea will always take its salt from the river.

All those things Wes knows to be true, but as he looks up at the wide night sky and sees not stars but the look in the eyes of his son when he'd reached for his outstretched hand and grasped only water, what he doesn't know and what he will never know is why all the times Maggie and he had made love they'd only made Benny.

Wes finishes the cigarette. In the scrubbing on the black sand beach he can hear Benny humming along to his hip-hop and in the lapping against the hull Leif telling him that sometimes it's a big king fighting at the end of your line and sometimes it's the line wrapped around the prop; what's important is that you know the difference and do something about it. Some things are certain but many are not. When dawn comes, he'll head to a spot where he knows the salmon make their turn for home and bait his hooks and lower the outriggers and unreel the lines, never knowing if he'll catch his limit or come up empty.

LONGBOARD

Bellman is straddling his board just beyond the breakers, the water swirling around him a sunset hue even though the early morning light is pale as sand. If you didn't know better you'd think it's a red tide, but the color's not an algae bloom. It's the reflection from his surfboard bottom and wetsuit legs. He's painted both traffic cone orange from a spray can he lifted from a Caltrans truck, Bellman thinking the trick to survival is not get mistaken for a sea lion.

"Bro," he says.

I paddle over. "How're they breaking?"

"Like a picture window. Haven't seen you lately."

"Work," I say, trying to focus on the pattern of the swells now, get the timing right, not think about patching together enough commissions on short sales and foreclosures so I won't lose my own house.

"It only is if it's work." He nods wisely to himself.

Bellman's dreads look like he popped up from beneath the kelp bed, but I know the streaks of gray aren't rimes of salt. The bell dangling from the hoop pinned through his left earlobe is showing some tarnish, too. It isn't how he got his name, though. I've known him since high school. One day word spread it was breaking 12 feet at Trestles and Bellman pulled a fire alarm so a bunch of us could ditch when they shooed us outside to line up on the blacktop in alphabetical order. The bell was still ringing as we gunned it for the beach.

"I only got an hour," I say. "Got to make the most of it."

He motions toward the noisy pack of juniors that always seems to be crowding the waves these days and then at the bluffs lined with condos that weren't there when we were their age. "It's all changed, Bro. We're longboarders in a shortboard world now."

I follow his gaze, thinking if it weren't for all those beige and white stucco boxes with their matching red-tile roofs spilling down the palisades like lava from a volcano I'd never have been able to put both kids in Hiddenbrooke Day, keep Debbie in the leased Lexus, own the timeshare over on Maui. Bellman? He's never buttoned down for a 9 to 5 in his life. Dropped out in 11th grade, started selling pot on the boardwalk while the rest of us took Mick classes and schemed to avoid detention. Once we took a road trip to Baja together. We scored some peyote outside of San Quintin from a guy who called himself a shaman and wore powder blue polyester pants so worn in the front they were nubbier than 60 weight sandpaper. We ate the buttons on the beach and it got so I couldn't tell the difference between the sparks shooting from the bonfire and what came flashing out of Bellman's mouth every time he howled at the full moon.

Bellman was never the same after that and then he disappeared for a while. When I finally saw him again, he was living on the streets, panhandling tourists, dumpster diving behind the Safeway. He pedals a Schwinn fat tire up and down PCH pulling a two-wheel cart with his neon board bungeed on top. Red and white plastic streamers flutter from the grips of the stingray handlebars that are jammed with clip-on side mirrors, squeeze-bulb horns, and thumb bells. In winter he sleeps in a graffiti-covered underpass that channels Salt Creek, beneath a lifeguard tower in summer.

"Here's my ride," I say.

"Take it easy, but take it." It's what he always says.

I swing the big board around as the glassy swell humps, give a few strokes, and then I'm stepping into it, planting a lazy turn at the bottom. I glide across the shiny face and drink in the sheer joy, taste the spray, ignore the young guys on boards half mine's size busy slashing and cutting on the shoulders, forget about the bottom dropping out of everything I know but the waves themselves. I think about walking it, cheat five, maybe even go for 10 over the nose, but then the tube closes out and I'm tumbling over the falls. No worries, I don't fight it. I wear an ankle leash now and the longboard always pulls me to safety.

Climbing back on, I think about catching another, but a glance at my watch sends me stroking for shore instead. I look over my shoulder as I paddle in. Bellman is still bobbing around out there, his face turned toward rays now growing stronger, yellower. He's got his arms outstretched mimicking a V of brown pelicans gliding just over his head. Above the sound of the surf, I swear I hear a tinkle. Bellman? What does he know about sales meetings?

***

The real estate office is in a storefront at the shopping center, the message being buying and selling a house is as easy as picking up a bag of groceries, trying on a new dress, outfitting the kids for back-to-school. Forget the meltdown. Ignore the mortgage crisis and all the foreclosures. You need food, you need clothes, and you need a roof over your head. Pick up a brand new home today.

Eight-by-ten color glossies of oceanfront trophies that no one can afford hang in the front window, but the real draw is Krystal, the receptionist, who sits at a glass-top desk with her hair just so and her breasts just so, positioned there as much for the wives as the husbands, her fun-in-the-sun look telling them, "Move here and you'll be slim and pretty like me," and, "Come on in, Hot Shot; I know you got what it takes."

She taps a long pink fingernail at the top of her forehead as I push through the glass front door. "You have a little piece of seaweed here," she says in a stage whisper. As I go to brush it off, she smiles to herself, the pinked lips smirking. "Got you."

"Everyone already here?" I ask, chinning toward the conference room at the rear of the office.

"Everyone but you." That's what Krystal says, but that's not what I hear. It's more like, "What do you think? They all play dolphin every morning and get dressed in the car on the way to work like you?"

"No worries," I say. "It's cool."

"Whatever," Krystal says with a toss of her head. A wave of just so blonde sweeps forward and I start thinking of what the surf will be like in a few hours.

In the conference room Reed stops what he's doing and gives me the stare. He's standing in front of a whiteboard squeezing an assortment of dry-erase markers like they're those spongy stress balls. The board is a color-coded roadmap to the office's annual sales goal. Only exclusives are listed. Reed doesn't waste ink on multiples with their split commissions. Initials represent the listing agent. Prices are written in green, days on the market in red. A closing earns a big smiley face drawn in Dayglo yellow.

He keeps up with the long look as I take my seat. "Glad you could join us," he says.

Reed's one of those guys who uses too much teeth whitener. The only time I ever saw him on the beach was when we had an office BBQ and he showed up in pressed Tommy Bahamas and tassel loafers with no socks. I asked if he wanted to join me bodysurfing and he looked like he'd stepped on a stingray. "Get real," he said, pushing past me. He's younger than me, I know it. Moved out from some place in the Midwest when the market went to hell and the agency got bought out by a big national chain that parachuted him in to take over as division manager even though I'd been there for more than ten years. I'm okay with it, though, considering what's going on with Orange County real estate, happy that at least the new owners don't make us wear gold jackets.

The weekly sales meeting is like all of Reed's meetings. He starts off as a kindly professor, carefully diagramming market forces with boxes and arrows, patiently explaining the latest move in the LIBOR, how the banks' strategic release of repos so as not to flood the inventory is actually good for us. Then he turns Sunday televangelist, pleading with us to give up our slovenly ways, to see the light, to find salvation in hustle, hard work, and a full six point commission. Finally, he's all football coach at half-time. Markers fly. Chairs get shoved and tipped over. The spray-on tan turns scarlet. The conference table takes a beating as he slams it while slamming us for being slackers and pussies.

Reed asks me to hang back as the rest of the agents scurry out. I know what's coming. It's not the first time. He takes a few deep breaths, tries to find the place that whatever the latest self-help book he's reading tells him is his potential just waiting to be tapped into. It's like the sales meeting all over again.

"You just don't get it," he winds up shouting. "Whatever thread you think you're hanging from is gone. Long gone. What was the last escrow you closed? That two bedroom shitbox over in the Terraces? Big whoop. It wasn't even an exclusive. You know what the office's take was? Not even the monthly on my C-Class."

I'm looking at him as he rants, but what I'm really seeing is Bellman sitting out there on his hazard orange board as sets of perfectly formed waves roll in: "It's only work if it's work."

"I'd've cut you long ago, but Debbie begs me not to," Reed is saying, his teeth glaring like the blank spots on the whiteboard.

If he thinks that's supposed to make me feel like some kind of loser, it doesn't. Truth is, my wife's been after me for years to give up real estate for software. Besides, Reed wouldn't stand a chance of making his sales goal without us. Debbie's the best stager in the business. A coat of Foam White semi-gloss for the trim and Beach Sand eggshell for the walls? Contrasting damask bedspread and high thread count linens on the rented bed in the master suite? Art books tastefully arranged on a glass coffee table brought in just for that purpose? Debbie can make a cramped condo look like a mansion. She could host her own show on HGTV.

And me? It's like riding a wave that closes out and sends me tumbling over the falls. I just don't sweat it. My ankle leash is the simple fact that I don't take a draw, only commission. I don't cost the agency a dime. And there's still plenty of people living here I know from back in the day. The recession's been hard on everyone. Most are downsizing, many are divorcing. I show up with a cold six-pack of Mexican beer, the coming week's surf report, and a sympathetic ear. More often than not, I leave with the listing.

"I'll remember to tell Debbie thanks for saving my ass tonight while I'm stroking hers," I say, getting up and heading for the door.

"Fuck you," Reed says right back.

"No, that's what Debbie'll be doing."

I didn't say those last bits, but I would've if I'd come up with them sooner.

***

Big, fat storm clouds are rolling in. The wind is whipping and the surf's blown out. Raindrops splatter against the windshield like I'm beneath a flock of overfed gulls. I've got a can of Modelo cradled in my lap and both hands on the wheel, but I'm not going anywhere. I'm just sitting at the edge of the parking lot watching the spume fly and the horizon play peek-a-boo between gray skies and even grayer seas. I've got a couple of hours to kill until I need to pick up the girls at Hiddenbrooke. Debbie's staging a Mission-style in Laguna Niguel and Reed asked me to attend a broker's open in Three Arch Bay, but who needs to shuffle through a 4 br w/ bonus room & whitewater vu cattle call now that there are 360 degree video clips online?

There was a time when I'd already be in the water, never missing a chance to take on a big storm surge when moon and tide cooperate and the current responds to the wind's lashing and the ocean sucks itself half way to Catalina before spitting it all back, the waves rushing fast toward shore one after another in steep, frothy walls as close together as whale ribs. Drop down one of those babies and the board chatters like giant's teeth, spanking the bottom of your feet black and blue, leaving your knees stiff for a week.

But now I'm okay just sitting in the minivan and watching. The way the waves are stacking up reminds me of a time off Capo Beach. It was probably a January, could've been a February. Anyway, a few of us are taking them on and someone yells "Outside," and I wheel around and see this monster charging straight for us, a really big, nasty cleanup. There's no time to get to shore and it's too big to dive under and all we can do is paddle right at it and hope to get up and over without getting caught inside. I'm clawing and kicking my way up, up, up that cold, dark face, trying not to think what's going to happen if it closes out, hurls me backwards, crushes me beneath its mountainous weight, when I finally shoot up through the crest, gripping the rails as tight as I can as I fly up and over the backside. I mean, I'm flying through the air, ten feet above the water easy, and I look over and there's Bellman right alongside me. It's like he's clinging to a rocketship flying right alongside me. It's like he's clinging to a rocketship and he has this crazy look on his face that isn't scared at all, just all "Wow, bring on it, motherfucker. Let's do it again."

And then, here he is, rapping on the passenger window of the minivan, his dreads plastered against his face in big wet clumps. He's wearing a green plastic trash bag like a poncho and the rain is just streaming off his shoulders. I reach over and unlock the door and he pours himself in.

"Bro," he says. "It's raining."

"Want a beer?" I reach behind to pull a cold one from the six-pack on the back seat.

And he says, "I'd rather have wine."

We sit there sipping from our cans and the minivan smells wet and funky and I've got to turn the defroster on because the windshield is steaming up. I'm guessing it's because of Bellman. God knows how many layers he's wearing beneath that greenhouse trash bag.

"You remember that time off Capo?" I say. "When the third wave of the third set rolled in?"

Bellman belches. "You got anything to eat?"

I pop the glove box and rummage around. I usually keep some Clif bars stashed in there for after surfing or for when I pick up the girls from soccer. I find one, but Bellman shakes it off.

"I got a bad tooth. Don't you got nothing softer?"

"Just the beer," I say. "When was the last time you saw a dentist? A doctor, for that matter?"

"I went to the free clinic in Laguna once."

"They help you out?"

"Nah, it wasn't for me. It was for this puppy I found. He had the shits."

"And the doctors at the clinic treated him?"

"Nah, they said take him to the pound."

"Did you?"

"Nah, they just gas 'em there."

"So what happened to the dog?"

"Shit himself to death."

I turn on the radio to a Classic station. It's playing Zeppelin, The Doors, Allman Brothers, and it brings it all back and I look over at Bellman thinking surely he's feeling it, too, but he's hunched against the door rubbing the side of his jaw. Even through his scrungy beard I can see a lump the size of a golf ball.

"Man, you got to do something about that tooth. How about I take you to our dentist? The girls don't even cry when he drills and fills."

Bellman shakes his head. "I'm gonna go see one in TJ. They don't charge so much down there, plus they're *muy* generous with the nitrous."

"Tijuana? How you going to get there? Ride your bike?"

"Nah, Bro. Soon as it stops raining, I'll just paddle on down."

We sit there listening to the music for a while and the rain comes down, banging on the top of the minivan like someone beating on a Jamaican steel drum. Maybe it's Page laying down licks on "Stairway," or Morrison singing "Riders in the Storm," or remembering the big wave off Capo. Or maybe it's just the couple cans of Modelo and thinking of Reed and all his color markers and sales charts, but finally I say to Bellman, "It's supposed to dump all week. I got a spare room off the garage. You can crash there and I'll drive you down on Saturday."

***

It's evening and Debbie's sitting on a stool at the kitchen island, a little blue light blinking at her ear and pictures of kitchen remodels flashing across her iPad as she flicks them from the screen like ants. I can tell from the combination of flirt and school mistress in her voice she's talking somebody into something. If she hears me come in, she doesn't bother to turn around.

"You know I'm right. It has to be a Wolf or Viking," she's saying. "It doesn't matter if the buyer can't even boil water. She wants all stainless, from the SubZero to the range. If she counts one burner less than six, you can kiss a sale goodbye."

I realize it's Reed on the other end and picture him trying to act cute by saying something like "kiss this," those teeth of his gleaming as he clinks the cubes in a V and T he's mixed at the full-size bar he built inside his Ritz Cove modern that Debbie's decorated in chrome and black leather. She's laughing now and I walk up behind her, put my arms around her and give her a squeeze. She doesn't miss a beat. She never does. She just keeps on talking, how she's going with an Island theme, going to rent a big white sectional for the living room, install plantation shutters on the floor-to-ceiling sliders. Fill the place with cut-glass vases of red antheriums and birds-of-paradise. Sure, it's going to cost, she tells him, but not as much as letting the house just sit there sinking deeper and deeper underwater, it being one of Reed's personal prospects, him picking up foreclosures, thinking he can make a killing flipping other people's heartbreaks in the latest California gold rush.

Debbie clicks her Bluetooth and the light flashes red. That's my cue. She spins around on the stool and I plant a big one on her lips. Debbie doesn't look a whole lot different than when I first met her. She was selling bikinis at Hobie's then and I'd come into the shop to check out the used rack for any longboards that might be going for a steal. One look at her was all it took. Two kids later and she can still wear one of those bikinis, those spinning and sculpting classes every week paying off big time.

She's working on a glass of Chardonnay and I top it off for her while pulling a bottle of Pacifico from the 'fridge. "Reed okay your plan?" I ask.

Debbie smiles. "He always does."

She gets a commission based on the sales price of every house she stages. "One of these days he's going to figure out you're marking up the furniture rentals and contractor fees, too," I say.

"Reed's the one who told me to do it, said I have to cover my risk. In this market there's no guarantee the house will ever sell." Debbie's frowning now. "Sometimes you're so," she gives it a long pause, "old school."

It's not the first time she's said something like that. After she quit working at Hobie's and started doing interiors and staging houses, I'd said it was too much work, what now with the girls and all. And she'd said right back, "When are you going to understand it's not about getting by, it's about getting ahead." That was right around the time we started leasing a Lexus. I don't mind driving the old minivan, though. At least it's got a good roof rack.

Debbie sips her Chardonnay then holds out the iPad. "Look at this," she says, giving the screen a tap

The designer kitchen disappears as a spread sheet takes its place. Debbie's good with numbers. She handles all our finances. "See?" She pushes it toward me.

"See what?"

She draws her fingers across the screen like opening a curtain and the numbers enlarge. I could see it just fine the way it was, but I let her have her moment. I start peeling the yellow and gold Pacifico label from the brown bottle, careful to get it all in one piece even though I already have one in my collection downstairs.

"This," she says, pointing at the skinniest column. "That's your income for the year." She lets it hang there for a while. "And this is mine."

Before I can say anything, a shriek comes from downstairs and the girls come thundering up. Ours is a split-level tract. Beige stucco. Red-tile roof. 3 br w/ bluewater vu.

"Mommy, Daddy. Mommy, Daddy. There's a creepy guy in the garage," the youngest is wailing.

"A real perv," the oldest says, trying to sound nonchalant and know-it-all at the same time.

Debbie's already punching 911 as she says, "Don't just stand there. Do something."

I wave the Pacifico. "Everybody calm down. It's just Bellman."

"Bellman?" Debbie spits it out like it's a bone in a fish taco.

"Yeah. You remember Bellman. I'm letting him sleep in the workroom for a couple of days."

"Dad," the oldest says, drawing it out like it's three syllables. "He smells really bad. He took off the front of the heater and is sitting in front of it. He stuck a hotdog on a coat hanger and is cooking it over the little blue flame. It really stinks down there. Honest."

I look over at Debbie and see that big, cold storm wave off Capo rushing straight at me. There's no time to get to shore and no way to get up and over it.

But Debbie surprises me. She coolly drains the rest of her Chardonnay and places the glass in the sink. She gives her hair a push back then runs her palms down the sides of her silk blouse and tight black skirt as if ironing out wrinkles. There aren't any. Then she grabs her purse off the granite countertop.

"I have to go. He better be gone when I get back."

"Where are you going?" I say.

"Over to the Dana Strand house. I have to take some measurements."

"Reed's flipper? This time of night?"

She looks pointedly at the iPad as if to say, "Do we need to look at those figures again?"

***

Some brokers would market my workroom as a Man Cave. I resent the label. Man Cave's are for guys who need to show off their full-size bars, huge plasma TVs, and maybe even a pool table. My workroom is just that. Sure, it's got an old TV and mini-fridge and classic surfing posters on the walls, a pretty good sound system, too, but it's where I go when I got work to do. Like repairing dings in my boards or patching my wetsuit, work on my label collection. Bellman is sitting on the couch. It used to be upstairs, but Debbie redecorated and said the plaid just didn't go with the new color scheme.

I pull a couple of cans from the mini-fridge and hand him one. He's staring at the TV, but it's not turned on. I lean against the workbench just looking at him looking at the TV, not sure how to start it off.

He's the one who finally breaks the ice. "Your old lady, she's pissed, huh?"

"What makes you say that?"

"I was eating when she pulled out and drove off. Gave me the real evil eye."

"This isn't a beach, man. You can't roast wienies over a pilot light. You could burn the house down."

"I don't know, Bro. I might've put it out."

"What, the heater?"

He shrugs. "You want me to split?"

I realize I'm squeezing the can of beer, just like Reed does those dry-erase markers. What the hell is Debbie doing going out so late, anyway? Measuring, my ass. I look over at Bellman. The lump on his jaw is red and angry. It's so swollen it looks ready to burst.

"No, you can hang out," I say. "I'll drive you down to TJ in the morning. You want to watch some TV? I got a re-mastered 'Endless Summer' on DVD."

I pop in the disc, grab some fresh brews, and join him on the couch. The girls are right. He really does smell pretty bad. I take to breathing through my mouth. We watch the film and even though I've seen it a hundred times the free-styling sequences and music still get to me. Bellman and I empty the 'fridge of all the beer and I'm thinking of our own surf safari we took to Baja all those summers ago.

"I gotta take a leak," he says.

"Outside," I say. "Don't splatter the flagstone. And don't let my girls see you, either."

I keep watching the movie and drinking beer and the next thing I know I wake up and the TV screen is lifeless and Bellman isn't back. I go outside, thinking maybe he fell in the bushes, but his bike is gone, too. I go upstairs and crawl into bed, but now I can't sleep, wondering where Bellman went, wondering why Debbie isn't back, either. She doesn't get home until two am. She takes a shower and slides in with her back to me. I turn on my side and put my hand on her shoulder.

"Don't," she says. "It's been a long day."

I never do fall back asleep. I'm up at dawn and strap my board to the top of the minivan and go looking for Bellman, thinking we can hit the prime spots on the drive down to Tijuana. Trestles, Ponto, Blacks. I check the Salt Creek underpass, but he's not camping down there. He's not asleep under any of the lifeguard towers, either. Maybe he isn't that out of it, after all, I think. Maybe he's riding his bike to TJ, him realizing pedaling 100 miles is going to be a lot easier than paddling, not to mention a whole lot safer. Then I spot his bike down at the end of the beach. It's leaning up against the seawall. There's no board strapped to the cart, no neon wetsuit shoved into the basket, just a bunch of greasy clothes and a dirty blanket. I see the footprints leading down to the water. I scan the horizon and see a dot way out there. It could be a boat heading south, or a gray whale. Or maybe a big raft of pelicans. But I'm pretty sure it's Bellman. I head back to the minivan, suit up, and grab my board.

You can keep your jogging, your free weights and membership at the gym, your spinning and sculpting classes, too. Me? There's no better workout than surfing. The truth is, I'm just more comfortable in water than on land. Back in school, I liked marine biology and that kind of stuff best. You know, anthropology, too. Learning about where we come from, how we evolved, how everything connects us back to some fish that figured out how to breathe out of water and grow hands and feet. I feel that way every time I run down the beach, throw my board in the water, jump on, and start paddling. Like now. Chin up, shoulders back, and just digging it, digging my palms into the water and scooping it like I'm scooping up dirt. I like crashing through the whitewater, climbing up and over the faces, slamming down the backsides, and just moving. Moving fast. Going out faster than the swells are coming in. Faster than the gulls wheeling overhead. Faster than the sparkles of sunlight dancing on the water.

I'm making good time, my eyes on the horizon, thinking about what Bellman's going to say when I stroke up beside him, him saying, "Whoa, Bro." I'm thinking about Debbie when she wakes up and sees I'm gone and the minivan, too. I'm thinking of Krystal and the little cut she won't be able to say to me because I won't be coming in late this morning; I won't be coming in at all. And I'm thinking of Reed and how pissed he'll be when he finds out and what he'll say when I come back. No, what I'll say to him.

I glance back to see how much distance I've covered and it's a lot more than I thought. The 3 br w/ bluewater vu is miles away. If Debbie and the girls are awake and looking for me through the telescope on the deck I'm not sure they'd even be able to spot me I'm so far out. It's going to take a couple hours easy to paddle back in. And then it hits me: I'm in a rip. The current is carrying me fast out to sea. I've been in rips before, but this feels like the mother of all rips. I don't even need to paddle, it's moving so fast. I think about everything I know about rips. How you can't fight them. How if you can't paddle parallel to shore to get out of them, then you just got to sit back and relax and go with it, knowing they eventually peter out. I wonder if Bellman's caught in the same rip, it carrying him further and further out, too. We get carried out far enough we'll run smack into the California Current and get swept south all the way down to Baja. A free ride. Hey, maybe paddling is faster than pedaling. Maybe Bellman isn't so out of it, after all. Maybe he's been right all along.

I'm feeling tired from all the brews the night before and the no sleep on account of thinking about what Debbie's up to and all the paddling. I put my head down on the deck of the longboard and rest my chin on the back of my hands. And as I drift under the yellowing sky, I stop thinking about open houses and listings and commissions, and start picturing sunny beaches where the beer's always cold and there are no beige stucco condos crowding the palisades. No short sales, no foreclosures. No skinny columns of figures. No trying to keep up with gleaming whiteboards and gleaming white teeth. No job. No hassles. No worries.

DENS

Summer thermals rising from the San Joaquin Valley prod the clouds bunched over the Sierra foothills, scattering them like spooked cattle. Tish keeps an eye out while driving along Highway 49, a winding two-lane that skirts canyons cloaked in silvery oaks and crosses rolling fields the color of mountain lions. As she slows going through an old gold mining town wooden boardwalks and weathered storefronts beckon. She parks in front of a hitching post that's not a meter and gets out to stretch her legs, find something cold to drink. Some of the buildings have historical markers with dates going back to the mid 1800s. Tish traces the raised lettering on a bronze plaque like it's Braille. The place is authentic, she's thinking, nowhere close to being a fake. Where she's coming from, she's had enough of those to last a lifetime.

A color printout of a ranch house for sale is taped on the inside of the front window of a real estate office that looks like it was once a saloon. The front door has a pick-head for a handle and a cowbell clangs when Tish pushes it open. She goes straight to the window and peels the ad from the glass. A plump woman in a white blouse with a red phone tucked between chin and shoulder stares from behind a roll-top desk. For a moment Tish wonders if she's going to chew her out for taking it down or maybe her baseball cap and sunglasses are not enough.

But then the woman says, "Call you back, Hon," hangs up and smiles. "Can I help you?"

Tish holds out the picture. "Is this still available?"

"Honey, everything up here is." The woman pushes away from the desk. She's wearing a patterned skirt that blares with green and blue philodendron leaves. "The name's Donna Bligh, but don't call me Captain." Her big hair bounces as she laughs. "*Mutiny on the Bounty*? Clark Gable? I just love the classics."

Donna plucks a business card from an antique gold pan that also shines with peppermint patties wrapped in tinfoil. The card has the realtor's picture on the front. The smile is the same though the hair isn't frosted anymore. Tish slips it in the back pocket of her jeans and Donna is off and running.

"Speaking of movies, people must tell you all the time you could be Tish Wiley's double. Don't get me wrong, I don't mean that in a bad way. You know, what she did and all. I mean your looks." She says in a stage whisper, "Personally? Her movies are a little too, well, they don't leave much to the imagination, do they? Larry, he's my husband, he brought a video home once and, I got to tell you, he got so worked up we nearly had ourselves number four that night." The big hair bounces. "Baby, that is. Three boys. Are they a handful. You have kids? Where are you from? Let me guess. L.A? Maybe San Francisco?"

Tish sidesteps by waggling the printout. "Could I get the address so I can drive by?"

"Hon, the only place your GPS will get you up here is good and lost. Come on, I'll take you myself."

"You don't need to do that," Tish says quickly.

"It's no trouble at all. And don't worry. I sell houses, not shoes. I'm not about to squeeze you into something that doesn't fit."

Tish hesitates as she decides between the usual excuses, but Donna is already grabbing a purse the size of a shopping bag and marching for the front door, talking about the hot weather, how she can't wait for summer vacation to be over, how she stayed up late last night watching *It Happened One Night* even though she's seen it a million times.

The Subaru Forester has a dented front fender and dusty back window. A pine tree air freshener dangles from the rearview mirror. Two more hang from the dashboard. They don't help much. Fast food wrappers and soccer jerseys litter the backseat. Donna's questions come like continuous forms spit from a printer as they head out of town on the two-lane then take a right on a narrow road that climbs between two hills and feeds into a gently sloping valley. Tish keeps her answers vague and her face turned toward the passenger window. A barbwire fence strung between wooden posts cracked with age runs alongside. Orange poppies open to the sun crowd the gap between the chip seal and a stubbly field dotted with bales of yellowing alfalfa. A flock of blackbirds loops and turns, shrinks and billows like a frightened school of fish.

Now Donna is going on about how most places out here are still working cattle ranches though some of the larger properties have been subdivided into what she calls hobby horse farms. They turn onto a gravel road and rocks ping the Subaru's wheel wells. Oaks line both sides and Tish pictures their thick trunks, checkered gray bark, and corkscrew limbs at dusk, imagines them silhouetted in soft, waning light, hears their branches sawing, their jigsaw leaves rustling as a hot summer wind blows itself out.

"The property runs a hundred acres," Donna says, waving a hand as she talks. She wears gold rings and bracelets on the left, all silver on the right. "It includes these pastures here and all the way up to the knob behind. There's an orchard of almond trees and one of peaches. They need some pruning, that's for sure. Someone tried a vineyard once, Zinfandel I think, but they weren't too serious about it." She hesitates. "It doesn't have a pool. Did you need a pool?"

The Subaru slows as the two-story house comes into view.

"I know, it's more *The Waltons* than Tara." Donna chuckles. "You must think I have a thing for Mr. Gable."

The house looks older than it does in the photo. The bones are plain and the sills and eaves in need of paint. Double-hung windows punctuate the top floor and Tish can see herself lying in a big bed made with fresh white linens and oversized pillows with morning sun streaming through newly-washed panes, a cup of tea balanced on her stomach. She can feel its warmth, smell the peppermint. The view from up there surely takes in all directions, she's thinking, and the nearest neighbors are at least a mile away. The house may be dated and worn, but it seems safe and secure. Just what she's been looking for.

***

Tish was born Marsha Williams and Link was Stevie Fleck. Names were easy to change; how they were raised took work. The only thing they liked about where they came from was each other, at least that's what Tish believed. She even said to herself "love," but never out loud. Link hated that kind of stuff, said so, said if you felt it you didn't have to say it, you just knew it, did it. Tish loved that about him. No, liked.

"I'm outta here," Link was saying.

It was his 20th birthday and they were lying on a mattress in his parents' garage that he'd turned into a studio for his band, his dad insisting that as long as they still had to put up with him living at home he sure as hell better keep the door down when he was playing covers of Nirvana and Sonic Youth.

"When?" she asked, tracing the tattoo of the tarantula over his heart, his areola the spider's abdomen. He'd gotten inked in Stockton at a parlor run by an old Vietnamese guy who wore thick glasses and always had an unfiltered cigarette burning. After making love–no, having sex, she reminded herself–she would touch the tip of each of the spider's legs, going around and around, imagining them as numbers on a clock, counting down the hours until she could leave home.

"Tomorrow, man," Link said. "I'm so done with this shithole's country music ways. They don't know Pearl Jam from strawberry." He reached over and shook a cigarette from the pack, lit it with a Bic. Blew the smoke straight up.

Tish was tracing the tarantula faster now, her fingertip skipping legs. "I know it's all we talk about, but…I just didn't think it would be right now."

"There's nothing holding me anymore. My old man gave me $200 bucks for my birthday along with the boot."

Tish pictured her dad, heard him yelling like he always did when she'd been out with Link, calling him a twisted little loser, saying his music sounded like it needed a brake job, that he should bring his guitar down to the shop where he worked and he'd put it up on the rack and check the shoes and drums.

"But I have six more months until I'm 18. My dad…" She buried her chin deeper into the crook of his arm.

Link shrugged beneath her, worked on blowing smoke circles.

"Joey going, too?" she asked.

"'Course. He's my bass. And he's got the truck. L.A., man. They won't know what hit 'em. Check it out. There's open mike at a half dozen clubs easy. The places Jane's Addiction and Hole got their starts. I mean, Courtney Fuckin' Love."

Tish had to fight to keep the words she wanted to say below the lump growing thick in her throat. "Okay, I can take the bus down on weekends. You can pick me up at the station. You know, use Joey's truck."

"Yeah, sure. Hey, check it out. The new stuff I'm working on? Starts off with fuzz then I bring in the loud. You know, all chord, no lyrics, building on it. And then I'm just, like, going 'Fuuuckkkk.' And then I drop it down into the quiet and give 'em the words." He bobbed his head then started singing, his voice weak and cracking, "*I'm standing on a hill, I'm all alone. I'm crying in the still, I'm so alone.*" He stroked the limp, dirty blond whiskers on his chin. "I mean, it's pain. It's hurt. It's so down there. I'm going to open with it first chance I get."

***

Tish notices there aren't any cars parked in front of the house. She says to Donna, "Doesn't look like anyone is home."

The realtor shuts the Subaru off. "It's a short sale." She shoulders the car door open and swings out with a grunt, her skirt hiking up in back, green leaves wrinkling into blue ones. "Come on, I'll give you the two-penny tour."

Blue jays scold from the oaks as they walk up the front steps to the wrap-around porch. No lockbox hangs from the door handle, just a key above the sill, no alarm to turn off inside, either. The empty living room is just off the entryway. Scuff marks streak the dark oak floors as if snails have been inside. The two women walk down the hallway, their footsteps echoing like the clopping of the unbridled horses Tish had stopped to watch earlier that morning.

She takes her sunglasses off as they enter the kitchen. It has new granite countertops, but the linoleum is yellowed with layers of old wax. The porcelain sink shows stains, though the faucet is shiny. "Some starts and stops at a remodel, I see. It's definitely had a few owners."

"It's had its share, that's true," the realtor allows.

Tish thinks of initials carved in a tree, people having to show they'd gotten there even if they couldn't stay. "Why? Is there something wrong with it I should know about?"

But now Donna is backing up against the opposite counter, her haunches sandwiching the rounded edge of the granite. She's staring and Tish can feel the air between them change, feel it the same way she felt the thermals lifting the clouds outside. It's all she can do to keep from putting her sunglasses back on. She glances around the kitchen to avoid Donna's stare, sees herself cooking a meal over the old-fashioned gas range she'd keep, washing dishes in a new sink she'd put in, standing on a new floor. No TV chattering in the corner. No cell phone ringing from the counter, just three placemats set at a country pine table, the glassware sparkling, the cutlery polished, the plates waiting for the healthy meal she'd cook herself.

Donna finally answers. "Well, I've been in this business a pretty long time and what I find it usually has more to do with the people than the house." Her words are measured now, not coming out in a rush like before.

"How's that?"

"We get a lot of folks coming here from the big city. They're looking to start a brand new life, but it's not always all they'd hoped it would be."

"You mean country life. Living in a small town." Tish nods to show she understands.

"There's that, but mostly it's because no matter how hard you try, the things you hoped to leave behind wind up getting packed into the moving boxes anyway."

Their eyes lock and Tish stiffens, knowing that Donna knows. "I'd like to take a look at the rest of the house, if you don't mind."

"Whatever you say, you're the boss."

The master bedroom is just like Tish hoped. The double-hung windows fill it with light and provide a clear, wide view of the surrounding countryside. The room has a ceiling fan and a water stain on one wall the shape of South America. That will definitely need primer, Tish thinks. The adjoining second and third bedrooms are cozy and share a bath. She stands between them and closes her eyes, hears a little girl talking to her dolls, a boy singing along to his iPod.

Tish doesn't say anything as she passes by Donna who's standing at the top of the landing with her back pressed against the wall. She walks downstairs and goes outside. A thick tangle of wild roses bows a faded white trellis. Overgrown parsley and basil sprout in the vegetable garden. Dry husks of last season's pole beans flutter from a limp net looped between two grape stakes. A shake-roofed tool shed is grayed by sun and has a lean. The chicken coop stands silent. It wouldn't take much to fence the entire property, she thinks.

Donna walks up behind her and Tish turns around. The sunlight makes Donna squint. Her big hair is collapsing in front and a few strands are sticking to perspiration dewing her forehead.

"I just have to ask you if you're...," she starts.

Tish doesn't wait. "I should have told you at the start. I

hope you understand why I didn't."

Donna nods, takes a deep breath, and then the words come tumbling out. "I wasn't sure at first if it was her, I mean you. I mean, well, when you first walked into the office, I thought, no, it can't be. What would she, I mean you, be doing way up here? We may be a hundred miles from anywhere, but we do get cable. The beauty shop subscribes to *People*. So does the dentist. But the people you read about, see on TV? Well, for folks like me, it's like you don't live anywhere but in those photographs, on TV." Donna takes another deep breath, sticks out her lower lip, and blows, trying to unglue the errant hairs sticking to her forehead. "But then here you are."

"Yes, here I am. But you shouldn't believe everything you read."

"I don't. Honest, I don't. But it's like I told you. I got four boys at home and one of them's my husband." She tries a laugh but blows air instead. "Then there's the PTA and church and showing houses. Sometimes it gets so busy I just want to stay in bed and pull the covers over me. Either that or run off to a tropical island." She tries another laugh. "I don't even want to imagine what it must be like to be you. Everyone at you all the time. Even before what happened. All those people everywhere you go. All the reporters and cameras."

"That makes two of us."

Donna sticks her hand out instinctively to pat Tish on the shoulder, but stops herself just short.

Tish feels it anyway. "Thank you," she says.

They stand there for a while, the blue jays scolding, the sun shining. Finally, Donna says, "Hon, I just want you to know, I, well, I always thought you were innocent. The bastard." She clamps her hand over her mouth as if to stuff the words back in. The silver bracelets jangle. "I can't believe I just said that. I'm so sorry, but, well I have children myself. Three sons. Did I tell you that already? Anyway, I just want you to know I don't blame you. Not one bit. When it comes to our kids, we're all mama bears at heart."

Tish no longer flinches. It's been awhile since she was in

court, even longer since being on a set, but she hasn't forgotten how to control her emotions, show them when it counts, hide them when she needs to. "You say it's a short sale? Does that mean a quick escrow?"

Donna visors her eyes with her gold hand. "You can't be serious?"

Tish nods.

"But why this place? Why up here? I mean, who you are, the trial, I'd think, well, you know, you'd be looking for a place somewhere like Aspen or France or Africa even. Some place beautiful and exotic and far away."

Tish takes in Donna's big hair, her gold jewelry on the left, silver on the right, the loud skirt that fit two sizes ago. She looks past her and takes in the orchards, the knob rising behind, the tips of tall grass rippling like wind across a pond, the glint of quartz streaking granite boulders. All of it is real, she's thinking. Donna. The house. The land. She takes a deep breath, tastes the peaches ripening on the unpruned trees, smells the waxy scent of pines drifting on warm air rising. There's something about this place that's unlike all the homes she does own in places like Aspen and France and Africa. And then it hits her. Not only does it remind her of the house she lived in until her mother died and her dad took her away, but it's surrounded by nature, close to the wild where things still are the way they were when they began.

"You know what you said about people wanting to start a brand new life? I just want my old one back."

Donna wipes her forehead, bites her lower lip. "Well, you know it won't be more than a morning at the Post Office before everyone in town knows you're living here. Not that I'd tell them. Honest. They'll just figure it out. My advice? First thing you do, Hon, you put up a gate out front. A really big one."

***

It was three months before Tish could get away to visit Link in L.A. As far as her dad knew she was on a camping trip with the senior class instead of a Greyhound that smelled of funk and

French fries, peering out the tinted glass as Modesto, Merced, and Bakersfield rolled by in a haze of burning fields. Link didn't meet her bus and she dug her fingernails into her wrist for imagining some kind of Windsong ad. She used a payphone to call the number he'd given her. The guy who answered said he was Joey's uncle and Link was out, but would be back later, seeing that he'd left his shit strewn all over the room he'd rented him. He gave her the address, told her she could probably take the RTD, but didn't know which route number.

Tish got on the wrong bus and ended up in Compton where the driver put her out, telling her he was going out of service, that she should cross the street and wait for a bus going back the other way, but this late at night they only ran once an hour or so. She took a seat on a bench with a billboard on it of a toothy man, a 1-800 number, and the words "Lawyer" and "*Se Habla Español*" in red letters. Cars drove by, some real slow, most with young guys who hung out the window and called to her. She'd never seen so many black people before, couldn't think of a single black person who lived back home.

A gray-haired woman pulling a two-wheel shopping cart shuffled by. She went about a half block, stopped, turned around, and asked Tish what she was doing. Tish tried to sound like she wasn't afraid, but the woman scoffed. "Girl, you mo' country than me when I left fo'ty year ago."

Tish told her about taking the Greyhound down, how Link wasn't at the station when she got there, how she'd gotten on the wrong bus, how all she could do now was wait.

The woman tsked. "Musicians. They all the same. Mine played trumpet. Played all night, slept all day. You bettah come home with me. My grandson's got hisself an automobile and we'll see about taking you to you music man."

When they dropped her off Tish thanked the old woman, told her she'd never forget her kindness, that if she could ever return the favor all she had to do was ask. She waved goodbye then knocked on the door. Joey's uncle answered wearing gray boxers. His stringy hair dripped onto bare shoulders pocked with acne scars. He ushered her inside. She followed him into a cluttered living room that reeked of beer and cigarettes and Chinese take-out. He plopped down on a sagging couch and patted the cushion next to him.

"Wanna watch TV?" His small eyes searched her.

"No thanks, I'll just wait in Link's room," Tish said.

"Whatever." And he hit the clicker, the screen filling with arching backs and thrusting hips, the room echoing with amplified moans and the slap of oiled skin.

Tish was exhausted from the bus ride, but spent the next hour straightening the dingy bedroom. No hangars hung in the closet so she just picked up Link's jeans and T-shirts and folded them into a neat pile. She dumped the aluminum beer cans that were torn in half and overflowing with cigarette butts into a brown paper bag with the name of a Chinese restaurant on it. When she was finished she sat on the bed cross-legged.

She dozed off and when she opened her eyes Link was standing in front of her, wired and weaving. "No fuckin' way," he said.

Tish forgot all about him not meeting her bus and jumped up and threw her arms around his neck, wrapped her legs around his waist. They tumbled onto the bed. He felt shorter and skinnier than ever. His face looked pale except for the black eyeliner that had leaked and streaked.

"Easy, man. Easy," he said. "I can't fuckin' breathe."

Tish was kissing his face, sucking on his neck, pulling at his shirt so she could get at the tarantula.

"Hey, easy," he said again, and pushed her away. He struggled to sit up on the edge of the bed.

"What's wrong?"

"Nothing, man. It's just that I'm wrecked. You know, playing music all night."

Link reached under the mattress, pulled out a cigar box. Tish sat up, too, rubbed her face on his shoulder, purred as he fumbled with the box. She heard the lighter flick, smelled the smoke, opened her eyes. He was drawing on a glass pipe, but it didn't smell like weed.

"What is that?"

He turned to her, clamped his lips around hers, and she thought she was going to taste his tongue but got smoke instead. It was cold not hot. She closed her eyes and pictured machine-made fog at a rock concert snaking down her lungs and up her sinuses and then felt a jolt like the time when she was six and had grabbed the frayed cord of a lamp at a cheap motel her dad had moved them into after her mom died.

Now the fog was a ghost and it was flying inside her and she could feel the blood racing through her veins, her toes and fingertips buzzing, her hair tingling. She wanted to stand up and dance, no, stand on the edge of a cliff like those divers in Mexico they showed on TV and just launch herself out into the deep blue sky and soar through the air then plunge into the deep blue sea. Everything all around her warm and liquid and shiny.

She opened her eyes. Link was on his feet clutching the pipe like a microphone, his head tilted, his mouth twisted as if in pain. "*I'm standing on a hill, I'm all alone. I'm crying in the still, I'm so alone.*"

He shook the pipe. "It's fuckin' unbelievable, man. All of it. Ever since I got here I been playing every night. Clubs here in the Valley. Garages down in the OC. Hanging with Black Flag, Circle Jerks. Did I tell you I jammed with this new band from San Diego? Stone Temple Pilots? Fuckin' awesome. I got a drummer and another guy playing behind me now, too. I'm going to make a video. It'll run nonstop on MTV. Duane – that's Joey's uncle – he owns this place. He knows lots of dudes in the movie business. Okay, they mostly do porn, but they're looking to branch out. They're going to start shooting tomorrow. Like, I'll just do whatever and they'll put it all together."

Tish realized the three months apart was as good as a year, that Link had left more than their hometown behind, that she was in danger of not being able to keep up, hang on. Link fired the glass pipe again. Tish watched as the ghost streamed out of his mouth and she jumped up to catch it in her own, not wanting any of him to get away, knowing right then and there that she'd have to hold onto him tight, that there was no way she'd ever get back on the bus, never go back to that little cold house and her even colder father.

"You can come watch me tomorrow," Link said. "I'll be up there playing. You know, lots of loud, lots of quiet, and right back loud. My chord work. My lyrics. Just feeling it. You know, the pain. The hurt. The really dark down there stuff. *I'm so still, I'm standing on the alone. I'm so hill, crying in the alone.*"

The lyrics lost, he broke it off. Tish put her arms around him, hugged him tight. She didn't need to stand on her tip toes to kiss him. "It's going to be great, baby," she said. "You're going to be great."

Link brightened. "Yeah, you're right. Tomorrow, that's when they're going to start shooting." He started bobbing. "And, hey, I'll let you be in my video, too. You can be dancing or whatever in the background. No, check it out, more like you're just zombied out by me and my song. Wearing something really sexy but dark. Whipping your hair back and forth."

He started dancing to some beat. "Yeah, everybody watching me. Listening to me. Who knows, maybe Steven Fuckin' Spielberg will see it. Not that I give a shit. I mean, who fuckin' cares about any of that. It's just about the music. That's what matters. You know, my art. But, hey, it's L.A., man. Anything can happen."

***

Moonbeams, oak rustles, and cricket chirps stream through the open double-hung windows. Tish is lying in her new bed, a warm breeze riffling the top sheet, summer still in the air. It's past midnight and she's waiting, listening. She turns to where the pale light shines on the stain of South America that still shows on the wall. The painter had rolled on coat after coat of primer, but they were never thick enough to cover it so she had him turn it into a design by adding the shapes of the rest of the continents. She used a small brush and painted blue stars on all the places that she had been, all the neighborhoods in L.A. she'd lived in, the locations from New York to Rio to Johannesburg she'd worked at, the film festivals in Europe she'd attended, the island getaways where fans and reporters were slow to follow, the houses she now moves between like a shell game.

The map tells the story of why she is where she is right now. She reaches out and touches the wall and traces the route from star to blue star, starting in L.A. where 20 seconds on Link's one-hit wonder led to 20 years of stardom for her. She lingers on all the stars where they had lived as she kept rising and he kept falling. She can hear all her cries and pleas, all his lies and rants. The star where the doctor told her the baby inside her had died because of drugs burns her fingertip. She sees in other stars all the rehab units, from the expensive suites paid by her manager to a grimy beige cell run by the State to the place where she hid so she could grow strong enough to finally forgive herself for losing the baby and get clear of Link, to resurrect her career. Then she skips ahead and touches down on Beijing where she finds in a bleak orphanage all that she'd been missing, the one thing in her life that fills the void that neither Link nor drugs nor acting could ever fill. Her name is Mai and she is beautiful. And then Tish's fingertip flies right back to L.A., passing over the ocean and the year in between, to the front door of a new house where, in a twist that even a script doctor couldn't dream up, the old woman from the bus stop of long ago now dying from cancer knocks and asks her to return the favor from all those years gone by. Save her grandson, she pleads, don't let the crack plague that has claimed his parents take him, too. His name is Alonzo and, just like his new sister Mai, he is beautiful.

Now, so many of the stars melt together as Tish sees days rushing by in parent teacher visits, sleepovers, birthday parties, holidays, roles with shooting schedules timed to school schedules, roles that earn her awards but never come close to the rewards her children give her.

A noise interrupts her, but it is not the one she's been waiting for. It's just the old house settling down for the night, the heat of the day finally loosening its grip on the wooden frame, the shake shingles, the oak floors. She turns back to the map on the wall and cannot avoid looking at the next to the last blue star on her journey, a home she and the kids were living in when Link came back into her life, a new Link, or so he claimed, repentant, reformed, renewed. Still unsure of exactly why, maybe to prove that not all of that part of her life had been a mistake, maybe to feel again what she had once felt so strongly, she invited him in. He'd brought presents for Mai and Alonzo, a new doll for her, an iPod for him. The reunion went so well that Tish invited him back, believing that maybe life had come full circle, that what she and Link had created together then lost could now finally be reclaimed. But it was Link who proved to be the better actor, at least until his mask slipped one night and in a rage blamed her for all that had befallen him, his failed music career, a stretch in prison, his ravenous need. And he threatened her, grabbed both her children, threaten to kill them right then and there if she didn't give him what she'd stolen from him, his money, his voice, his songs, his fame.

A roar pulls Tish from the memory and sends her springing out of bed to the window. It does not frighten her, not like the first night she'd heard it and ran to gather Mai and Alonzo from their beds and locked the doors and windows to her bedroom and called Donna for help. Donna, whose bracelets jangle and big hair bounces, telling her it was only a mountain lion, probably a female with newborn cubs, that Tish was living with nature now and wild creatures dwelt there, too, that she, more than anyone, should understand.

The lioness roars again and in the cry Tish hears the truth. She peers into the night to see yellow eyes glowing back, a tawny coat rippling, a dark-tipped tail twitching. She has a pair of cubs so young they still have their spots and she's moving them from one den to another to keep them a step ahead of danger and out of the reach of bobcats, other lions, and men. But should the new den be discovered by any who stalk her, and should they gain entrance by force or guile and threaten her cubs, she'll stand her ground and slash with claws as sharp as a carving knife frantically pulled from a kitchen drawer and plunged deep into a spot indelibly marked over the heart again and again.

Tish stands at the open window watching the wild creature that shares more than the night with her. The summer wind brushes her skin and tugs at her thin nightgown. The corkscrew limbs of the oak trees wave and shadows of clouds sail silently across a moonlit sea of grass. Only a few more hours remain until daylight and then Mai and Alonzo will wake and she'll make them breakfast and clean the house and do whatever it takes to keep them safe, either here or there, until they are grown and gone.

TOMORROWLAND

The Prez says to the new kid, "Go on. Touch it."

Andy has to think about it before he does.

"See, you don't feel no specks, no orange peel, no *nada*."

Andy can't. It's Pearl White and the luster so deeply layered he wonders if he might sink up to his first knuckles before reaching metal.

The Prez revs the Lincoln's 462 a final time then shuts it down, Andy now thinking it looks like a cumulus but sounds like a thunderhead. The Prez slides out of the deep rolled leather seat and stands beside him in the employee's parking lot behind Benning Paint & Body in Anaheim.

"*Bonito*, no?"

Andy knows enough to know he's supposed to say something. It's expected. "How long did it take?"

"A week. A coat a night. I hand buffed every spray." The Prez deepens his voice. "And on the seventh day he rested." He may be smiling, but it's hard to tell. The outlines of goggles and a respirator mark his face like tan lines on a skier and the pores on the tops of his cheeks and forehead resemble the color chip samples in the front office showroom. "The boss, he gives me the booth at night. Lou's okay as long as you punch your eight and buy your own color."

Andy isn't sure what to say next. "Looks brand new. What year is it?"

"A '66. I got her off a repo last year." He takes a deep breath then exhales the next two words long and slow, "Lincoln Continental." He pulls a Newport from the pack. "I don't drive nothing else."

"Was it in a wreck?"

"Factory original. Like a virgin. The owner drove her new off the lot just couldn't keep his payments up."

"Three years old, but you still painted it." Andy says it out loud even though he's saying it to himself.

The Prez lights up, twin streams of smoke exiting his nostrils. Andy glances at the Lincoln's dual chrome pipes. "A plastic surgeon don't have scars. A tailor don't dress in rags. I'm an artist, *ese*. My ride is my canvas."

Andy reads the red-on-white stitched nametag above the blue uniform's right breast pocket. "Diego." It's only his first week on the job, but already he knows no one calls him that. It's *Presidente* or The Prez. None of them working the line call each other what their parents had named them. The fender guy is Guitar. Manny the sander goes by WD, short for Wet 'n Dry. The striper? Well, everybody calls him Paco. Who knows what's on his ID, or if he even has one? Andy considers what they'll call him, wonders if he'll be there long enough to earn a handle.

"So, what do you want to be? Not a metal pounder. A sprayer like me, right?" The Prez, posing with the Newport dangling from his lips, runs his palm over his hair. It's still Elvis in the front, but the back is definitely leaning Santana. Overspray from the Riviera he'd painted Silver Metallic that morning dusts the 'burns.

"I'm not sure."

"What's that supposed to mean?"

Andy makes The Prez for 30, maybe 35. No way he can understand. "I'm taking some classes at Santa Ana JC couple nights a week."

Now The Prez looks disappointed. He pulls a chamois the

color of butter from his back pocket and wipes the suicide doors even though they're spotless. "College Boy, huh?"

Andy doesn't give a shit about school. Truth is, he doesn't give a shit about anything anymore. He's just counting down the days until December 1, going through the motions ever since they changed the game, they saying it was fairer this way. Most of the time he feels like he does two hours after smoking a joint – eyelids heavy, legs even heavier. If one of the first 100 little blue plastic balls pulled from the glass bowl contains a slip of paper with his birthday on it, well, maybe, just maybe, that article in the *Freep* will be right. Maybe having enrolled in JC that fall will be his ticket out. Far out, he thinks. Far fucking out.

"Well, let's see how smart you are, College Boy." The Prez drops the butt on the asphalt, doesn't make a move to grind it out. "'Cause here? The only thing you can scratch is your *cojones*. Cars come out of the booth so hot you feel your reflection before you see it in the shine, you don't even want to breathe 'less you fuck it up. You see the Lincoln Continental?" His stare hardens. "No runs, no drips, no errors. I got a rep and you got to do your part."

Coffee break over, Andy heads back inside the cinderblock garage and begins peeling masking tape and brown Kraft paper off the windshield of a Bel Air that's now Sea Mist Green.

"He showed you his wheels, huh?" Jaime looks up from the Chevy's bulbous headlights. He's scraping the overspray off with a razorblade and wiping the glass and chrome down with a red shop rag soaked in solvent. "That Lincoln's a piece of shit. Everything Ford makes is. You know what Ford stands for?" He covers his nose and mouth with the rag and huffs. His eyes scurry behind the droopy lids then peek back out. "Fucking Awful Ride, Dude."

When the shop boss had introduced them, Jaime told Andy to call him "El Cid." "Like the movie." He explained he'd thought the nickname up himself after seeing it on the ABC Sunday Night Movie. "I'm following in my uncle's footsteps. El Greco. He used to be the head sprayer here until he got Tboned by some old lady running a red over in Fullerton. Everyone knows he's the best there ever was. Ask anybody. Here, up in L.A., all the way out in the Valley. They'll tell you. El Greco? Nobody comes close. The Prez? A *maricón*." Jaime slapped himself on the chest. "El Cid. Ask anybody. I look just like him."

And Andy had said, "Who? Charleton Heston?"

Now, as Andy pulls the rest of the paper off the Bel Air the two maskers walk by. They're the only women working at the shop besides the bookkeeper, who Jaime says Mr. Benning is banging even though he's married and you could hide one of her Parliaments in each of her wrinkles. The maskers favor bright mascara, tight Capri pants, and pink low-top Keds. Rolls of manila tape ring their wrists like bangles. The couple of days Andy's been working there he already sees they spend 15 minutes in the bathroom before leaving work each night, ratting their hair and switching into high heels.

"Hey, Sydney. Why hasn't your friend asked me out yet?" the tall one calls. "He's *muy guapo*."

"It's Cid, not Sydney. El Cid. And I'll show you *guapo*." Jaime grabs his crotch. "You want some more of this? You know you like it. You know where to come find it."

"I'd got to find some glasses first." She pauses, giving it a full 30 seconds before adding, "El Cindy."

The short masking girl laughs.

Jaime wolf whistles as they walk around the spray booth. "That Marcia chick, she likes to lap fuck me in the back of my Monte Carlo." He takes another huff from the solvent-soaked rag, his eyes flickering. "Ask anybody."

Andy doesn't say anything, but he's pretty sure Jaime drives the faded blue Nova with the coat hanger antennae and rear-ended trunk.

***

They're like that Russian's dogs they'd taught about in biology his junior year, only it's the roach coach ahoogaing as it screeches into the parking lot at both coffee breaks and lunchtime that signals them to come running. Andy's been working at Benning's three weeks now and it's a glazed donut and Styrofoam cup of watery coffee every morning, a burrito and Coke for lunch, and a Twinkie in the afternoon, sometimes a Hostess Cupcake. He's making 50 cents over minimum, but leaving two hours of pay with the driver every day. He doesn't care. What's it matter anyway, with D-Day coming on fast now?

"Hey, College Boy. They don't teach you how to read at your school?" The Prez is alternating swigs from a bottle of Orange Crush with drags on a Newport as the rest of them swarm the catering truck, both sides of its customized camper flipped up like silvery wings on a beetle.

Andy unwraps the tin foil from a beef and bean burrito, already knowing where the conversation is headed, knowing it means he'll have to scarf standing up. "How's that?"

The Prez waves his filtertip in the direction of the employees' cars. "The want ads. You thought you read they was selling a Corvette but you drive home in a Corvair." Again, it's hard to tell if he's grinning, what with the outlines that aren't from the sun.

Andy wanted to buy a VW Bus, but Aunt Ellen is letting him drive her '63 Monza. It's the least she can do since she moved into the two-bedroom with him and his mom following her divorce. Besides, she never leaves the couch and her Tom Collins's anyway.

The Prez takes another swig of Crush. The soda makes him look like he's wearing lipstick, or maybe it's just the weird light caused by the sun trying to burn through smog so thick Andy can barely make out the top of the Matterhorn towering across the Santa Ana Freeway.

"You got to drive it, at least let me spray it, *ese*," The Prez is saying. "What is that pussy color anyway?"

"Saddle Tan." Andy says it without hesitation. Not beige, not sand, not off white. But he's not really listening to The Prez anymore. He's doing what he always does when he's in the parking lot, looking at the Matterhorn, wondering if his birthday comes up on the slip of paper will he wind up flying over real snowcapped mountains to get where they'll send him. Mount Everest, he's thinking, it's somewhere over there, too. The only time he's seen the Matterhorn up close was when his dad was still in the picture. The ride had just opened, but they wouldn't let him on a bobsled because he wasn't as tall as the minimum height line on the Mickey sign. His dad boarded without him and, after the ride, for the rest of the day, couldn't stop crowing about how cool it was, telling Andy the Tea Cups sucked, the Dumbo ride was for little girls, and asking why couldn't you buy a real drink here?

The Prez says, "How about Palomar Red with a pinch of gold dust thrown in? That'd look sharp. *Muy fuerte.*"

Walking back inside, Jaime says to Andy, "You gotta be shitting me. He's got no eye. Ask anybody. You can't be thinking red with that interior unless you want to spray the dash and pop for new vinyl and mats, too."

Andy doesn't reply, still thinking about soaring mountains, but Jaime can't let it go. "If I was you, I'd go Daytona Yellow with a black competition stripe like they do on the Camaro. Either that or the Chestnut Metallic or the Nugget Gold on the new Toronado. The Nugget don't come stock. You got to order it factory special."

Andy glances at the wall clock. It's the same kind as in every classroom he's ever sat through. Big numbers and the slowest hands on Earth. "The Mustang's ready," he says. "I'll get it."

He places his palm on the spray booth's double doors. The heat no longer bothers him. He even likes it, likes opening the doors and feeling the blast hit his face, the billowing gases blowing back the loose strands of hair not held fast by the rubberband. He tries to imagine a snowcapped volcano blowing its top, but what he really sees is a steamy jungle and what he really hears is the whop-whop-whop from the big green helicopters he always hears when his mom and Aunt Ellen are watching the evening news. Andy tears a face-sized hole in the brown paper taped over the windshield. The Prez has left the driver's side door ajar, the jam freshly sprayed

British Racing Green, too. He can feel the metal buttons on his Levi's heat up, pictures them glowing red and leaving a row of singed circles on the fly of his Jockeys. He slides into the bucket seat, the back of his T-shirt sticking to the black leather. The masking girls have wrapped the key head with a couple of extra layers of tape, but it still burns his fingertips as he fires the ignition and eases out of the booth, using the heel of his palm to hold the hot steering wheel straight.

Jaime's waiting with a silvery blade in one hand, a damp red rag in the other. "I'm serious, man. You got to let me spray your car, even if it is a fucking Corvair. I got to build my rep. Show Mr. Benning my talents. I got plans. I ain't gonna be a detailer all my life. Ask anybody." He takes a hit on the rag.

Andy peels the rest of the paper from the windshield, rolling it as he does, careful to pull the masking tape cleanly from the rubber seal. "You're not worried about getting drafted?"

"What you talking about?"

"The draft. You know, the war? How old are you anyway?"

Jaime sticks his chest out. "I'm gonna turn 21 in January, man. They haven't sent me the notice so far so I don't think about it no more."

Andy balls the paper up, lobs it at the metal can. Two points. He starts on the Mustang's side and back windows. "It's all changed. They're going to do it by lottery now. You know how it's going to work, right?" When Jaime gawps, Andy explains how they're going to pull numbers out of a hat every December, but this year being the first time, they're going to include everybody up to age 25, not just the 18-year-olds. He wads up more paper. "Some kind of fair." The ball caroms off the rim and skitters across the concrete floor.

Jaime dresses the wheels with tire black then pops the Mustang's trunk to do the spare. "So what? I ain't gonna sweat it. There's nothing I can do about it. And if they do call me up? I'll tell 'em I want to paint Jeeps and tanks and shit. That'd be cool."

"There's always ways." Andy checks the glass for overspray.

Sometimes the maskers miss the corners. "You ever read the *L.A. Free Press*? The *Freep*?"

Jaime shakes his head. "L.A.? No, man. I don't never go up there."

***

Even the shop boss is calling him College Boy now. Lou asks Andy to work the stockroom after deliveries, partly because he thinks since he's going to school he can figure out the numerical filing system and partly because he doesn't need a step ladder to reach the top shelf. The stockroom is narrow and poorly lit and a maze of crowded wooden racks. Headlights and grills and moldings go on the right, paint on the left. Though the gallon cans are arranged on the shelves by factory code, whenever The Prez comes to get one he never asks for it by number, as if saying anything less than the names thought up by marketing guys in Detroit would cheapen what he does.

Andy is in the back restocking a case of Fleet White when the tall masker comes in. As always, she looks like she just finished putting on makeup. He wonders if The Prez sprays it on her every morning.

"I need a couple rolls of extra-wide," Marcia says.

By now he knows she means Kraft, not tape. The rolls go on dispensers fitted with serrated blades fixed atop wheeled carts. Marcia and the other masking girl push them around the newly-sanded cars as they work, tearing off just the right length of paper, taping it down so fast their long red fingernails blur. Watching them wrap the bumpers and door handles reminds Andy of the window displays at Buffum's at Christmas.

"Here, I'll get it for you."

"That's okay. I know where they are."

Marcia walks toward him. She's wearing hoop earrings and a gold crucifix hangs from a thin chain. Perfume fills the cramped room like wind blowing through the groves of orange trees that haven't spouted tract homes yet. It covers the scent of enamel and thinner. Andy huffs it and holds his breath.

"Don't worry, I don't bite," she says with a smile that

reveals a crown the same color as the cross.

Andy feels the hard edges of the shelves pressing into his shoulders, not realizing he'd backed up. He tries to think of something to say, but realizes it would just sound dumb.

She reaches next to him, her fingers brushing his bare arm, and slides a roll of Kraft from the shelf. "You like working here?"

She's standing so close he feels the buttons of his Levi's burn like when he's in the booth. "I like detailing better," he stammers. "You know, there's more room to move around. Than in here."

Marcia smiles. "I meant all of it – working here at Benning's? You're not going to stay when you get done with school. I mean, that's why they call you College Boy. You're getting an education so you can work in an office. Be a lawyer or a doctor or something."

"I could go to Vietnam." It comes out so fast he can't even believe he said it. He hopes he doesn't sound like he's gung ho or a wimp or worse.

Her face doesn't look so shiny anymore. Now she's holding the roll of Kraft to her chest. "My fiancé's over there," she says softly. "Five months now."

"Oh, I didn't know you were engaged." He can hear how it sounds so he tries to cover quickly. "And he's in the military and all."

"Well, sort of engaged. I mean, not official, with a ring and stuff. But Danny and me talked about it right before he shipped out. He didn't have time to buy one, but we talked about it, all right." She's nodding to herself now.

Andy wants to say he believes her, but what he really wants to know is what 'Nam's like. "Have you heard from him?"

Marcia's clutching the paper even tighter against her chest. It's pushing the collar of her blouse aside so he can see the white bra strap against her skin. Aztec Bronze, he thinks, '66 Impala. Her mascara darkens, her lipstick frowns. "Danny's not too big on letter writing. Me, neither. We weren't too big on school." She gives a little laugh. It sounds like his mom's canary, Frankie; she didn't know if it was a boy or girl. "He called me once, though."

"They have phones over there? You can call home?"

She nods, her thick, black hair partially covered by a red kerchief knotted in the back. "But they don't work too good. I mean, I didn't even recognize his voice when I answered. It made him sound like, well, he sounded like a little boy."

Andy hesitates. He's hearing his dad now, the time they were at Disneyland and his dad bought a balloon, but instead of giving it to him he untied it and sucked the helium out of it and started talking like Mickey, laughing so hard at himself that his eyes watered and snot leaked from his nose.

"Did he say what it's like? What they have him doing?" It's all he can do to keep from asking if he's been shot at, shot anyone.

"Danny said he didn't want to talk about it. Ever."

They stand close to each other in the gloom of the stockroom for a few minutes, not saying anything, Andy focusing on her hair and makeup and earrings, trying to block out thoughts of shadowy figures in conical hats carrying guns.

Finally, Marcia says, "I got to get back to work." She waves the roll of Kraft at him. "Thanks."

"Sure," he says. "Anytime. I mean it."

When she gets to the door, she says without turning around, "I guess it's because it's so far away and the phone line is so long. You know, why it makes you sound like, well, not yourself."

***

It's only a couple of weeks until D-Day and Andy is going into work earlier and earlier, doing everything he can to stretch it out. Now that he's the first to arrive the shop boss gives him a set of keys so he can open up, unlock the chain-link gate at the entrance, and roll up the metal doors to the bays. Andy's the only one there when a tow truck honks to let him know he has a drop-off. He goes out to show the driver where to park it, a black GTO still hanging from the hook. The front end looks like a missing slice of pie, the empty sockets that once held headlights staring cross-eyed. The front windshield is spidered, the passenger side darkened by a hole that looks like someone chucked a basketball through it.

"It's totaled for sure," Andy says to the driver who's now out of the wrecker and hitting the lever to release the cable. "Why didn't you take it straight to Aames?" Meaning the junkyard in Placentia.

"Fuckin' A, but tell that to the fuckin' insurance company. Doesn't mean fuckin' shit the driver and his passenger are fuckin' DOA. They think you drop a fuckin' nuke you can still sweep the mess up for under the fuckin' $500 deductible. Fuckin' adjustors."

Andy can't take his eyes off the wreck. "They're dead? They got killed?"

The driver unhooks the GTO. It settles onto the blacktop like a horse kneeling down, the blown front tires cupping the bottom of the mags. "Usually what fuckin' happens when you're going 90 and overshoot the fuckin' offramp and hit a fuckin' pylon." He puts on the *Get Smart* accent. "Missed it by that fuckin' much."

After the wrecker leaves, Andy circles the GTO, a scarlet patch beckoning from the rear window. At first he's scared it's blood, but then he sees it's a decal of a red bull with yellow wings, underneath it the lettering, "Marine Corps Air Station El Toro." Seeing it, he hears the nonstop thunder of the F-4's practicing touch and go's that rattles the apartment day and night, hears his Aunt Ellen cheering from the couch as she sucks down another Tom Collins, "That's the sound of American freedom, Buddy-boy. Love it or leave it."

He has to yank it hard, but Andy is finally able to wrestle open the driver's side door. He slips into the bucket seat without knowing why. The custom steering wheel is bent. There's a brown stain on its chrome spokes that isn't rust. He flips down the visor. Stuck in the registration held by spiral bands is a photograph. A guy in a flight uniform holding a helmet stands in front of a jet fighter and stares back, his devil-may-care grin saying, "Fuck you and the horse you rode in on."

Above the Hurst stick shift is an 8-Track mounted beneath the dash. The key's still in the ignition. Andy turns it to ACC and the tape deck whirs and *Voodoo Child* begins blasting from speakers mounted in the doors and behind the rear seat, picking the anthem up in mid-chord. He looks back at the photograph, seeing how it played out last night, the jet jockey racing down the Santa Ana to get to the next bar before last call, the music pounding, his flight buddy in the bucket seat at his side playing air guitar. They're laughing, singing along. Nothing can touch them. What's going 90 when you've gone 900? Had they already seen action or were they just finishing training and about to ship out? And what were they doing listening to Hendrix? Guys like that, the ones who are always the quarterback, they didn't go for rock. Beach Boys, maybe, but Jimi?

Rapping startles him. It's the fender man. Guitar taps the window with his scarred knuckles again. Andy tries to roll it down and turn the key off all at the same time. The music dies, but the glass is stuck in the buckled door frame. He shoulders the door open. The hinges groan and metal on metal grates.

"What the hell you doing in there?" Guitar growls.

"Sorry, I was just looking for, uh, any paperwork. You know." He knows it sounds lame.

"Sorry? Whoever was driving this is the sorry sucker. Those teeth on the floor mats?"

Andy can't help himself and looks down. "The tow truck driver says they were killed. It's a total, right?"

Guitar takes a step back. He wears a flattop ducked in the back and cocks his head as he looks the GTO up and down like a critic appraising a sculpture. "Frame's bent, front end's gone, firewall's got to be split from the engine slamming into it, and the block's also got to be cracked. Oh, yeah. It's parts now."

"The driver's a Marine fighter pilot," Andy says, chinning at the photo staring back from the visor. "I mean, was."

Guitar glances at it. "Now, if that isn't totally FUBAR." He straightens and salutes the car. "*Semper fi.*"

Guitar's forearm is corded with muscles from years of swinging bumping and finish hammers. Andy takes in the tattoo of a bulldog with a studded collar and the four initials below it. "Were you at El Toro, too?"

"Strictly a Grunt. Camp Pendleton. It's where I shipped out to Korea. How I wound up coming back to live in So Cal. Best days of my life, big time. Worst days, too. Not counting any of my marriages, of course." His laugh sounds like he's got a sore throat.

Andy keeps looking at Guitar, trying to see what's different about him now that he knows he's a former Marine, still seeing the dead guys driving the GTO, wondering what it was all of them had, what even his dad who'd fought the Germans had, too. What was it that he didn't?

Guitar is looking right back at him. "You haven't served, have you?"

Andy shakes his head, suddenly aware of all his hair. "Not yet, but we'll see in 13 days."

The fender man rubs his jaw with his thumb, the nail the color of bruised fruit. "Word of advice? You get a low number, don't wait around. Run straight down and sign up. The guys they draft? They get rat-fucked, big time. Take it from me."

***

Though most of them bitch, they all show up. They got Thanksgiving Day off, but it was back to work the next day, and now it's the usual half-day on Saturday. Andy would punch in tomorrow if they'd let him, Monday being D-Day. He would've come on Thursday, too, holiday or no holiday. It would've beat sitting around the cramped apartment watching his mom drip tears on the turkey his dad wouldn't be there to carve, listening to Aunt Ellen go on about how she couldn't wait until Christmas and the Bob Hope Special, and didn't she look just like Joey Heatherton. Andy didn't answer, not because of her weight, but because all he could picture were the guys in their hospital beds giving the thumbs up, those that still had arms and knew what planet they were on.

Andy and Jaime are finishing their third car of the day, a '65

Vista Cruiser painted Viking Blue. It's taking them longer than usual to detail because of the station wagon's chrome luggage rack and all the tinted dome car glass. Still, they don't break for lunch as they always work straight through on Saturdays 'til the 1:30 punch out.

"I can't believe Olds took a cherry ride like a Cutlass and bolted a piece of shit like this on it," Jaime says. "It's disrespectful. Something those Ford fuckheads would do. Ask anybody."

"They're going to start pulling numbers at dinner time, but they're in Washington so we could still be at work when we find out," Andy says.

"What are you talking about?"

"The time zone difference."

"Hey, man, daylight savings already ended. Like a month ago."

Andy doesn't know whether to laugh or cry. Before he can do either, the shop boss walks up. Lou tells them as soon as they finish the Vista Cruiser to knock off for the day. That everybody's knocking off now, that Mr. Benning bought a case of beer and they're going to have a little Thanksgiving celebration of their own out in the parking lot.

"Mr. Benning gonna pop one open with us?" Jaime asks.

Lou, not bothering to keep the "what a dumbshit" out of his voice, says the owner has a family commitment, and goes to tell the others.

Jaime says to Andy, "Meaning him and the bookkeeper are already checked in at the Disney Hotel doing it Donald Duck style every time the monorail goes 'round." He huffs the rag and quacks.

"How about I finish this one up," Andy says. "I'll catch up with you outside."

Glad to be alone, Andy takes his time. No overspray misses his eye. Not a strip of tape stays hidden to the underside of a molding. He polishes the bumpers and hubcaps until they're mirrors.

"You're going to be late," Marcia calls in a sing-song voice as she and the short masker push out of the bathroom, their hair, no longer covered by kerchiefs, ratted and bouncing like tumbleweeds. Andy sees they've put some swing into their hips now that they've traded their pink Keds for high heels.

"Almost finished," he says.

But he's not. He comes up with more things to do, even using a narrow brush to dress the whitewalls. Finally, the Vista Cruiser spotless and sparkling, he reluctantly turns off the shop lights, rolls down the bays' doors, double checks the heavy brass Yale locks then heads for the parking lot.

They're all standing around an opened cardboard box like it's a campfire. The four doors of The Prez's Lincoln are open and Boss Radio, KHJ, pounds from the speakers. The Real Don Steele is spinning them, mostly Marvin Gaye and Aretha with some Steppenwolf and Rascals thrown in. Guitar grabs a can of Coors, pulls the tab, and flicks the ring into the air. "What took you so long? They're not getting any colder."

He hands it to Andy. Andy stares at the gold can for the longest time, then chugs it.

The Prez, impressed, slaps his shoulder. "Now, that's the real pause that refreshes, right College Boy?"

Andy just nods and grabs another can and chugs it, too. In no time, he's got a ring tab on his pinky and ring fingers of his left hand, another beer in his right. He doesn't say much, just grooves to the tunes and the masking girls' whispers and giggles, ignoring Jaime's lame comments and The Prez and Guitar talking about the Rams chances for another title now that Rosey Grier has gone Hollywood since wrestling the pistol away from Sirhan Sirhan.

Lou is the first to split, telling them to make sure to lose the empties and close the parking lot gate. As soon as the shop boss is gone, WD pulls a joint from the pocket below his stitched nametag, thumbs a stainless steel Zippo, takes a hit then passes it to Guitar.

Andy can't believe it; he never would've guessed the ex-Marine for a head, figuring out now why his voice is always hoarse. Guitar tokes on the joint then hands it to The Prez, who puffs it like one of his Newports, exhaling through both nostrils. Jaime's standing right next to him, but The Prez passes it to Marcia instead, who pinches it with her red fingernails and holds it delicately to her red lips.

"Hey, what about me?"

The Prez, his eyes now sparkling like he forgot to wear his goggles while spraying a metallic job, says, "You got so many fumes coming off you, you'd go up in a ball of flames. Have to call you El Cinder." Everyone laughs.

"It's El Cid," Jaime insists, his voice cracking. "How many times I got to tell you that?"

He stomps over to his Nova. It takes a couple of cranks before the ignition catches. He tries to burn rubber on the way out, but the engine is thumping like it's missing in at least one cylinder and the smashed-in trunk lid yawns as he bounces out of the driveway and onto the street.

They finish the joint, laughing every time one of them imitates Jaime. After a while nothing seems that funny anymore and the beer is gone besides. Guitar crushes his empty. "I'm out of here." He glances at Andy, both his face and that of the bulldog on his forearm look expectant. "You remember what I told you about not waiting?" But Andy just stares down at his shoes.

WD and Paco soon follow, leaving Andy, The Prez, and the maskers closing the circle around the box full of empty cans. The girls are making dance moves in place as KHJ plays on. Andy notices how strong Marcia's calves look beneath her black Capris. When the music gives way to a read-through of the headlines, The Prez says a little too loudly, "You're going to get a high number, *ese*, two, three hundred for sure."

"He's right," Marcia says quickly. "Don't worry about it. You'll see." She leans into Andy, squeezes his arm. Her hairspray and perfume overpower the lingering burnt broom smell of the weed and he wants to go on smelling it forever.

It's still afternoon, but the sky is darkening. Maybe it's from the smog, maybe it's from the dope and the beer, Andy isn't sure, but across the freeway it looks like clouds are gathering over the Matterhorn.

The Prez says, 'You feel okay, College Boy? You look a little pale."

"I'm okay," he says.

"Okay enough to drive?"

"*No problema*," he says.

The Prez shoots him a grin. He's got a Newport going now, not a hair out of place. He puts got one arm around Marcia's waist, the other around the short masker's shoulders. "I'm going to give the girls a lift home. You okay closing up?"

Andy wants to say no, to tell Marcia not to leave, that he'll give her a ride home, but all he does is nod okay.

"We'll see you Monday, then," The Prez says, winking.

He steers the masking girls to his Lincoln, putting Marcia in the front seat, the short one in the back. The Prez closes the suicide doors. He gets behind the wheel then leans out the window. "And what about Tuesday? You going to be here, too?"

Andy thinks on it. "Guess that depends on Monday."

The Prez tilts his head for a moment then nods to himself, fires up the big 462, and they glide away, his hand dangling out the window, his fingers flashing the peace sign.

Andy watches them go. When he can no longer see Marcia's reflection in the side mirror he turns back to the Matterhorn and just stares at it for he doesn't know how long. Finally, he decides what he's going to do. Not on Tuesday, but right now. He's going to get in his Corvair, slap in the 8-Track he lifted from the GTO, crank Jimi up full blast, head across the Harbor Blvd. overpass and into the parking lot on the other side of the Santa Ana, go up to the booth and buy an E-ticket, and when the bobsled reaches the top of the snowcapped mountain, he's going to raise his arms so as not to hold on, and maybe he'll laugh, and maybe he'll scream, but, for sure, he's going to keep his eyes wide open every twist and turn the whole wild ride down.

PIPEWORK

Cold dirt hidden from the sun for more than a century lies beneath JT's back. Joists sawn from a redwood ten times as old run above his face. A foundation made of cement mixed with sand dredged from the Oakland Estuary surrounds him. Three stories that for generations held the dreams of a single family and now those of strangers in need of cheap rent stand over him. Eighty tons of hardwood floors, lathe and plaster walls, and second-hand furniture in all, but the house is as light as memory for all JT can feel.

The pain that had seized his chest is gone leaving everything numb. The steady drip of water that splashes in his eyes as it leaks from the old cast iron pipe he'd sought to stanch goes unwiped. Only the sounds of the living coming from overhead tell JT he is still among them. Floorboards creak as Mrs. Collins shuffles around her first floor unit in bedroom slippers. Heat ducts hum with hip-hop from Jesse and Eduardo's boom box as the couple sweats through their morning workout routine on the second floor. Even the whispers of the shy exchange students living in the converted attic echo down here in the crawlspace, the old house's uninsulated walls transmitting their voices as clearly as if they were Skyping their parents half-way around the world.

This isn't JT's first heart attack, but it's nothing like the one he'd had the year before. That was so mild he'd chalked it up to the flu or maybe a bad burrito he'd bought off a lunch truck. He still refused to believe it even after Martinez drove him to the Doc-in-the-Box on Telegraph Ave., Martinez being the old plumber who'd taken him on and taught him the trade when his sculpting fell flat and hunger won out over art. After the doctor gave him the news, JT said he must be reading somebody else's chart because he was way too young for something like that. When he fled the examining room, he found Martinez snoozing on a green vinyl couch beneath a wall-mounted flat screen turned to ESPN. JT told him there was nothing to worry about, that he was fine and wouldn't miss a day of work. "What does a drive-in doctor know anyway?" he said. He hadn't smoked for years, gave it up when he was still sculpting and a pack hit $5. He was already eating oatmeal a couple of times a week. True, it was instant, but still. And no way he was going to take a pill every day that cost $10 a pop, not without insurance. Martinez said he was glad to hear it and asked if he wanted to grab a bowl of chili up the street.

Now JT's thinking that Mrs. Collins and the other tenants are going to think he's pulling a Martinez, the old plumber always the one to volunteer to shimmy under the house because he liked the cool, dark quiet, especially on hot summer afternoons. "Gonna take me a little *siesta*," Martinez would say, patting the top front pocket of his brown Carhartt bibs where he stashed a plastic flask of peach brandy the color and smell of kid's cough syrup, it as much a tool as his spud wrench and channel locks. But JT works alone these days and there's no one to tap him on the thick white rubber soles of his Redwings to let him know it's time to wake up and get back to work. No one to ask if he needs any help switching out a line, replacing a valve so they can finish up and get to the next job on time. No one to pull him out by the ankles when they realize he isn't napping.

JT stares at his right hand. It's frozen to the red handle of the pipe wrench he was using to tighten the coupler joining two lengths of pipe, his fingers mimicking the tool's metal teeth still clamped to the joint like a pit bull's bite. He wonders why he can't let go, can't make his arm or shoulder budge, either. Despite the beam from his Made in China headlamp, his hand and the wrench keep drifting in and out of focus. It's like looking through one of those half-walls made of glass blocks the rich women want built around their walk-in showers these days. There's something on the other side, for sure, but the Coke bottle bottom-like glass makes you have to imagine what it is you're trying so hard to see.

JT knows he's got to unstick his hand before he can drag himself across the crawlspace to daylight and call for help, dial 911 on the cell phone he left on the front seat of the Econoline. He concentrates harder now, trying to push though whatever it is that's swaddling him like overalls and a hoodie soaked by a burst main. If the right hand don't work then try the left. That's something Martinez would say when he was flat on his back with his head and shoulders stuck in a cupboard trying to get at a hard-to-reach fitting beneath a kitchen sink. So JT tries wiggling his left fingers. Half is better than none. That's another one of Martinez's, what the old plumber would say when wrestling a stubborn valve. It takes a few tries just to lift his left hand off his chest to make a grab for his right. Finally, he's got hold of his wrist, but as he pulls pain shoots, lights flash, darkness blinks.

Only it isn't the cheap headlamp that's flickering.

***

The first time he met Martinez JT was picking through a rack of used three-quarter inch galvanized at a salvage yard in West Oakland. The old plumber listened politely as JT told him he was looking for material for a piece he was sculpting.

"You making a man on a horse, you could use 6-inch drain for the legs, an old water heater for the body. Mount an oval sink upside down for the head," Martinez said.

JT explained it wasn't that kind of a sculpture. He described what he had sketched out, a human skeleton of pipes spouting used motor oil and affixed with broken pieces of mirror from a bathroom vanity. "It's part of an environmental installation series I'm doing. The pipes are veins, the mirrors greed."

"You sound like you gone to college," Martinez said.

JT nodded, thinking of the MFA he'd earned at California College of the Arts just up on Broadway, the four years he studied engineering over at Berkeley before that.

Martinez rubbed his chin. "How much you charge by the hour to build something like that?"

When JT admitted there wasn't much money in art Martinez said, "Well, it's all in the eye of the beholder and sometimes people just don't see so good. Now, you take what I do. No matter the economy, people still gotta drink, still gotta flush."

And that afternoon JT found himself going on his first job as a plumber's apprentice, riding shotgun in Martinez's boxy white Ford Econoline with Martinez & Sons lettered in Old English script on the panel sides. JT worked a month before asking how come he hadn't met any of the sons yet. Martinez glanced at the clouds and crossed himself. "I always hoped for them, but sometimes even the best of plumbers hooks 'em up wrong and you wind up running cold instead of hot."

JT could tell the first time he went to the big house on Vernon Street where Mrs. Collins lived that it was Martinez's favorite customer. That's how the plumber talked. Houses were customers, people clients. He called all the old places in the Adams Point neighborhood "Grande Dames." Most had been built right after the 1906 earthquake by frightened San Franciscans. Martinez revered their heavy porcelain sinks and claw-foot tubs, respected their cast iron pipes, mollycoddling them if that's what it took to keep them flowing. He only replaced old with new when there was no hope, no replacement parts to be found at the salvage yard. Whenever one of the big places fell to flames or a wrecking ball, he'd mutter, "That ain't no way to treat a lady."

As they got out of the Econoline, Martinez said to JT, "The whole family used to live here, but then all the kids run off to the suburbs and they turned her into a triplex. They may have cut her up, but thank God they didn't tear her down." And he crossed himself.

When Mrs. Collins answered the heavy front door, Martinez gave a gallant sweep of his short-billed pipefitter's cap and introduced JT. "Mrs. C runs the roost here. Her grandpa built it. A big insurance mucketedy muck from 'Frisco."

Mrs. Collins looked to be a grandmother herself. She was tiny with red hair that had gone a few weeks without a touch-up and wore a royal blue velvet bathrobe and thick pearl necklace. JT wasn't sure if it was a cataract or a contact that sparkled in her eye when she cooed, "Oh, Mr. Martinez, I don't know what we'd do without you."

She ushered them into a sitting room with twin gold upholstered chairs and a matching settee. JT was no expert but he was pretty sure all the furniture was Victorian, maybe Edwardian. The dark paneled walls held heavy-framed portraits of unsmiling men in stiff collars and women with big hats and lace. Thick drapes blocked the windows and oriental carpets covered the floor. The eye-sting of cat piss mixed with that of mothballs. The light was awfully low, but not enough to hide the fray.

"I don't see a leak in here," he whispered to Martinez.

"Take a load off," the old plumber said good-naturedly as he sat down on the settee.

JT tried to fit himself into one of the curved-leg chairs, afraid he'd break it. Mrs. Collins tittered like a schoolgirl watching him. "I'll just go get the tea, but big strong men like you, you'll be wanting a real drink."

Before JT could protest, Martinez said, "Whatever you say, Mrs. C. And you know you don't need to waste no ice on us."

After the old lady disappeared, JT said, "We're not on the clock yet, right?"

Martinez shook his head. "This is what you call your public relations."

"But what about the leak?"

"Lots a times Mrs. C calls, the only thing leaking is her eyes when she gets to thinking on the late Mr. C or her kids that don't never bring her grandkids around for a visit. Once they even forgot to come collect her on Christmas."

Mrs. Collins returned pushing a black lacquered tea trolley, only there was no teapot, no tea cups. Instead she ferried in two cut-glass tumblers filled with a thick, dark amber liquid and a dainty stemmed crystal cordial so fragile-looking JT couldn't believe it didn't shatter with each rotation of the wobbly wheels. Mrs. Collins positioned the drinks right in front of Martinez and sat down close beside him. The old plumber did the honors, handing her the cordial and passing a tumbler to JT.

"Well, here's to the grandest of the Grande Dames and I'm not just talking about the house." Martinez winked.

"Oh, Mr. Martinez. You are such a charmer," she said, her rouged cheeks reddening.

The drink was syrupy and way sweeter than JT expected. He hid his grimace as he gulped it down and placed the empty tumbler back on the trolley.

"Tasty, huh?" Martinez said. "Crème de Cacao. On Sundays Mrs. C serves Crème de Menthe."

"I'll let you two catch up while I go look at the plumbing," JT said, desperate to find a sink so he could get rinse out his mouth.

"Take your time," the old plumber said. "But careful you knock on any doors before poking your head in. Mrs. C has her reputation to think of so she only rents to ladies and that includes the pair living on the second floor, if you catch my drift."

***

JT is staring straight up. It takes him awhile to realize the giant amoebas swimming above him aren't real, aren't spots behind his eyes. His headlamp is casting shadows of the dripping water on the subflooring. JT's right hand is no longer stuck to the wrench handle. He wonders if the cost of freeing it was another heart attack because he's pretty sure he blacked out for he doesn't know how long and the tang of bile fills his throat.

He knows if he pukes he'll choke before he can roll onto his side. That is, if he can roll.

Dragging himself to the distant square of daylight on the far side of the crawlspace that marks the open trapdoor seems out of the question now, he's so exhausted. All that's left to do is yell for help, yell so Mrs. Collins will hear. But she may have left her hearing aids sitting on the nightstand so he'll have to yell loud enough for Jesse and Eduardo to hear over their hip-hop. He can picture them looking down from their window and seeing the Econoline parked out front, realize what's happening, come down and shine a flashlight into the crawlspace. Okay, Jesse will be the one to stick his head into the opening and shine the light. He'll spot JT, tell Eduardo to calm down and call for the fire department, call for an ambulance.

Help is such a small word, JT thinks, a simple word, but it's like trying to reach an engagement ring that's slipped down the shower drain. When he tries to grab hold of it, all he gets are echoes, garbles coming from deep inside him. And then it strikes him. He might die down here before anyone misses him and comes looking, the realization so clear now it cuts straight through all the other clutter, the jumbled thoughts in his head, the heavy numbness swaddling his arms and legs like soaked coveralls.

The headlamp blinks then dims, making him think of a piece he once sculpted. He'd jig-sawed two sheets of plywood into the shape of a man and woman holding hands. Then he drilled holes all over the standup figures and fitted them with salvaged light sockets and screwed in different colored bulbs. He wired them all to a transformer equipped with an elaborate timer he'd engineered himself so that the lights blinked on and off in a carefully choreographed sequence to spell out word pairs like fear and anger, hopes and dreams, happy and sad, love and hate. It was his final project for his MFA, part of a group show with the rest of the graduates. When it was his turn, he stood beside his sculpture and flipped the transformer's switch, but something went wrong and all the lights came on at once then blinked off in rapid succession without spelling anything as gray smoke curled from the electrical box. Instead of applause and an earnest discussion of his piece's social relevance, all he could hear was laughter and all he could see was the dismissive look on his girlfriend Callie's face as she turned and walked out of the gallery with another grad student who'd already had a one-man show in San Francisco, a painter who talked and smoked like Javier Bardem.

Now his own lights could be blinking off for good, JT is thinking, and the only thing left shining beneath the house will be the faint square of daylight at the trapdoor. Eventually, he knows, that, too, will extinguish as night comes before anyone comes looking, before anyone finds him, before anyone tells him they have seen his sculptures and calls him an artist, tells him she's sorry and loves him.

***

Jesse's skull was shaved and gleamed like Mrs. Collin's polished black lacquered tea trolley. Eduardo was lithe and wore a short kimono after their morning workout. It was a few weeks after JT's first heart attack and he was watching them as they stood on the other side of their second floor kitchen island, the centerpiece a chrome multispeed blender. Wire baskets filled with fresh fruits and vegetables hung like wind chimes and old-fashioned apothecary jars holding organic wheat grass, vanilla whey, and green max powder crowded the countertop.

"Your body's a temple, man, you got to worship it," Jesse was saying as he fed carrots, celery, and spinach into the whirling blades. "You got to stop eating that shit you and Martinez buy on the street. I can hear your arteries slamming shut from here." He glanced to his left. "Careful, 'Duardie, you don't cut your finger off slicing those kiwis like that."

"Oh, stop," Eduardo said, affecting a dramatic eye roll. He turned to JT. "He just can't help himself. Worry, worry, worry. You should have seen him when I was with the Ballet and he was working sets backstage. Just a big bundle of nerves. You'd think he was the one out there making pas after pas."

"Yeah, and look what happened the one night I did turn my back," Jesse said.

Eduardo grimaced and shifted his weight as if suddenly one foot was pressing down on broken glass. "You don't have to remind me."

Jesse poured soy milk into the whirring blender. "Three years we worked trying to get him back. Surgery. Rehab. PT. Acupuncture. You name it." He shook his hairless head.

Eduardo stuck his chin up and held his arms aloft, a plate of fruit in each hand, as he glissaded over to the dining room table. "'I coulda been a contendah.'"

JT grinned even though he'd heard Eduardo's imitation before. He joined him at the table as Jesse brought over a pitcher of smoothies the color of a newly mown lawn. Coming upstairs while Martinez visited Mrs. Collins downstairs had become his own form of public relations. The first time JT knocked on their door, Eduardo had clapped his hands and called out, "Oh, goody. A singing-telegram. Go ahead, big boy, take it off. YMCA me." JT was stammering he was only Martinez's apprentice looking for a leak when Jesse came up and told him Eduardo was just joking.

Now when he visited, he and Eduardo commiserated about what it was like when you could no longer dance, no longer sculpt, how you filled your days, whether or not you could ever be satisfied tightening pipes, unclogging toilets, selling organic honey and working the cash register at your partner's health food store.

"When are you two going to realize all that existential shit doesn't mean shit," Jesse said as he sprinkled flax seed on his fruit salad then drizzled coconut oil over it. "What's important is how you treat yourself. Healthy body, healthy mind. You feel good, you feel good about yourself. Who you are." He speared a piece of mango and slurped it from the tines like an oyster.

"Oh, puh-leez," Eduardo said. "Now you're suddenly Sinatra? *Do be do be do?*"

Jesse pointed his fork at JT. "You tell me. You don't get satisfaction fixing someone's plumbing? Helping them out, solving their problems? You ask me, there's plenty art in that."

JT skated the tall glass around, making the green froth on top swirl. "I suppose."

"You know I'm right." Jesse turned back to his plate. "You got a job, you got helping others, you got love. What more's a body need?"

"Still working on that love part," JT muttered, trying to forget the memory of walking into the San Francisco gallery and seeing the huge canvases of Callie posing nude alongside the bio and headshot of that Bassett hound-eyed painter from grad school.

"You got all the love you need right here, man, you just open your eyes to it. Aren't I right, 'Duardie?" Jesse said.

Eduardo puckered his lips green from the smoothie and made air kisses.

"Take Martinez. How long's he been driving that old van? You think he finally painted out the 's' in Sons now that you're working with him 'cause he suddenly found a spare can of white? And Mrs. Collins. She told me those girls upstairs finish the semester and go back to Seoul she'll let you move right in even you being straight and all."

"If that's not love, I don't know what is," Eduardo said, patting his lips with a napkin. "You're part of the family."

***

The shadowy shapes swimming across the subflooring are becoming human figures now. JT can see Callie, her hair raven, her skin pale but for the bracelets of red hearts tattooed around each ankle, naked like in those canvases hanging in the gallery, naked like when they used to sleep together. He met her the first year at art school when they had studio together. By the end of the semester she'd moved into his loft in the Market District with Seaweed, her little brown dog that barked at his sculptures and snored on their bed while they made love. JT wants so bad to talk to her, to tell her that he truly loved her, that he hopes whenever she feels a breeze while looking at a sculpture, sees a shadow moving across it, she'll think of him.

But he can't form the words to say all that, as speechless

now as the time he'd run into her at a Diebenkorn retrospective. JT had taken Martinez to the Oakland Museum, telling him the café there served turkey and pesto sandwiches on sourdough, talking up the taste, not mentioning they were healthier than their usual greasy lunch. JT wolfed his and left the old plumber at the table so he could take in the show. He spotted Callie standing in front of a row of canvases from the painter's Ocean Park series. She was cradling her little dog like an infant. JT thought about what he was going to say, but when he went over, Seaweed bared his pointy teeth and growled. Callie showed no surprise at seeing him. She spoke as if he were just another visitor looking at the same painting. "What I like about Diebenkorn is what he doesn't put on the canvas. I'm free to fill it with whatever I want. I see what can be, not what can't." She was stroking the top of Seaweed's head, a new tattoo encircling her wrist; it was the signature of the guy who painted her nude. "His art's so liberating, know what I mean? He's not someone who wastes his time focused on what he hasn't done, what he doesn't have."

JT knew who she was really talking about. She always complained he was negative. Before he could say anything, Martinez walked up. The old plumber studied the row of paintings. "You ask me, guy musta been pretty lonely. Not a picture of a house or people anywhere, if you catch my drift." He brushed some sourdough crumbs off the bib of his Carhartts. "You ready to go? We got that customer up on Adams needs her hot water heater fixed."

Callie sidestepped to another painting without glancing back. JT thought about going over, telling her that he'd seen the nudes and they certainly didn't evoke a picture of freedom to him, not with all the forced poses, gags, and knotted ropes, that the guy who painted them was about as real as the guys Javier Bardem played in the movies, that she was bound to get her heart broken, too. But then he started thinking about the Grande Dame with the broken hot water heater and how she needed him to fix it, that there were all sorts of things he could try, like check for an air bubble, clear the lines of calcium deposits, replace the thermostat. So he left, following the old plumber across the museum and out the door.

Now the shadows and faces on the subfloor fade away as the headlamp falters. It's getting so dark JT can barely make out the drips from the leaking pipe. He closes his eyes and feels water trickling down his face like tears, feels them like the time he sat next to Mrs. Collins on the gold settee in her dark paneled living room and gently held her blue-veined arthritic hands while he told her that Martinez wouldn't be stopping by anymore. Hearing her as she said between sobs, "Oh, JT, I don't know what we'll do without him. He was such a charmer." Hearing her say would he like a glass of Crème de Cacao and would he please sit with her a spell, asking him if he she'd ever told him about her grandchildren.

The last time JT had seen the old plumber was the night he drove him home after a 10-hour day replacing copper pipes in a Grande Dame on Perkins. Martinez had insisted they work straight through, not wanting to leave the clients without running water overnight. He even passed on taking his usual *siesta*, working side by side with JT without taking a break.

They sawed off old pipes streaked with patina like that on old metal-clad church steeples, the elbows riddled with pinholes caused by faulty grounding. They hung lengths of replacement pipe as shiny as new pennies underneath the house and ran them up through the floors and walls. The work was hard and tedious, but JT liked it. He liked planning out the way the system would all be connected, creating a spiderweb of copper veins that allowed water to flow uphill. He liked figuring out all the measurements, all the angles, cutting the lengths precisely, matching the right elbow fitting to the degree of the obstacle the pipe had to go around. He liked deburring the inside of the fittings and cleaning the outside edges of the connecting pipes so they'd join together snugly. He liked painting on the flux with a thin brush and positioning the tip of a length of solder wire against the joint as he held the blue flame of the propane torch to it. He liked watching the copper change color as it heated and glowed and the solder liquefy into shiny beads that quivered like quicksilver as they hurried to fill the seams.

As he did all that, JT knew Jesse had been right after all.

When they had finished and the customer's pipework was flowing again and the client could go to bed knowing that her faucets would work and the toilets would flush, JT and Martinez went to a bar across from Lake Merritt to celebrate. They sat on stools and had shots with draft backs while the A's lost to the Angels in hi def above.

"I ever tell you I wanted to be a ballplayer?" Martinez said.

JT shook his head while signaling the bartender for another round.

"I was pretty good as a kid. No, better than good. I played short and could hit the long ball, too. There was kids' leagues all over the city back then. We played in the parks and the local stores would give us uniforms with their names on the back. Tenth grade I caught the eye of the coaches at Bishop O'Dowd. You know, the big Catholic school up there on Stearns where the *padres* spend more time on the diamond than they do in the classroom. Anyway, they was going to give me a scholarship and bring me over there for my last two years. Set me up to be scouted and recruited by the bigs."

"What happened?"

Martinez glanced at the ceiling and crossed himself. "My old man caught cancer that summer so I went to work construction for my uncle instead."

They watched the game for a while, sipping their beers. During a commercial JT said, "You ever look back and think of what could've been? Any regrets about not playing ball?"

Martinez held his shot glass between bar and lips. "Not for a long time. Besides, it worked out for the best anyway." He downed the shot and chased it with beer. "You know the difference between baseball and plumbing? Devil takes all the ballplayers 'cause there's never a rainout in hell. Plumbers? They go straight to heaven. God needs all the help he can get when the clouds start to leaking."

Usually after a job JT would walk back to his loft in the

Market District or catch a bus. But that night Martinez asked JT to give him a ride. "I'm beat," the old plumber said. "And that was even before them drinks. You keep the van tonight and pick me up bright and early. We got two, three jobs stacked up for tomorrow. It's like all the fine ladies in Adams Point need their hair done at once."

JT, seeing that Martinez was unsteady walking out of the bar, held the passenger door open for him, worried that the old plumber might teeter backwards as he hoisted himself into the front seat. They didn't say anything on the ride across town. Martinez lived in a tidy neighborhood east of Fruitvale Ave. where all the stucco bungalows on the block kept their Christmas lights strung up year round.

When they pulled into the driveway, JT said, "You need a hand?"

Martinez shook him off. "Nah, I'm fine, just tired. Real tired. The wife's still up. She'll have dinner waiting along with a few choice words." Before shutting the Econoline's door, he said, "You did good today. Kind a job that makes you proud. Real proud, if you catch my drift."

***

JT opens his eyes. The drip is still dripping, the headlamp still dimming. It takes effort to move his hand, but he reaches up and switches off the light. It takes even more effort to turn his head to the side so he's facing the open trapdoor on the far end of the crawlspace. Maybe it will be Jesse who comes to fetch him or maybe it will be Martinez. As he waits, he stares at the small patch of daylight that's the color of a blank canvas and looks for all that he did do, all that he does have.

CHARIOTS

The new guy says call him Ajax, that everybody does, but Stremmel's thinking he's got his brands mixed up, what with the shaved head, gold hoop in his ear, and the size too small white T shirt and matching pants. He's even riding shotgun in the specially equipped van with his arms crossed genie style.

"Like the soap?" Stremmel saying it like he doesn't believe it as he concentrates on the traffic. The 405 out of Long Beach is starting to jam up and they're running late as it is.

"No, the Greek warrior."

"You mean Achilles."

"That's his cousin. They never laid a glove on Ajax. Nothing ever wrong with his feet."

Stremmel checks the rearview mirror. His passengers are sitting in wheelchairs secured to the floorboards with holdfasts. He gives the new orderly a sideways glance. "Who told you that?"

"I got DISH. They throw the History Channel in for free. Some of the shows are pretty good. Like this series on war? One episode's just about tanks." Ajax uncrosses his arms long enough to pound a palm with a fist. "Boom."

Stremmel pictures George C. Scott as Patton slapping a leather riding crop against his leg. He checks on the passengers again. Bullets got some, IEDs the rest, but none are there because of tanks, Saddam's armor being flattened in the first 24 hours and the Taliban and al Qaeda never having anything heavier than Toyota pickups, if you don't count the airliners.

Ajax crosses his arms. "Another episode was about the Trojan War." Now a dopey grin is widening his already wide face. "I know, like the rubber. Anyway, they showed this picture of him. Well, a picture of a marble statue. Dude was huge. Had a sword was as thick as a 2x4, a shield the size of a car door. A Mercedes."

Stremmel nods. "And you're sitting on the couch munching a bag of Doritos and see your reflection in the flatscreen and think, hey, that's me." He puts the blinker on and changes lanes.

Ajax scrunches his face until his brow ridge nearly swallows his eyes. "Wasn't me thought it. Was my mother. Says I weighed 11 pounds the day I was born. Starts calling me Ajax after watching that show. Now everybody does."

"You live with her?"

"No way." Ajax saying it fast. "I'm just racking there until I get my own place. You know, since my discharge."

A Honda whips into their lane forcing Stremmel to slow down. He checks the rearview again. Some of the guys are napping, others playing with their phones. Tollson, the youngest, is looking out the window with his thousand yard stare. They're all wearing gray hoodies and sweatpants, or in the case of the legless, sweatshorts.

Stremmel says to Ajax, "You served? What branch?"

"Army."

"Active or Guard?"

"Guard."

"Where?"

"Over there."

"Doing what?" He doesn't bother to mask the doubt.

"Logistical support. But we saw plenty of action."

"You mean loading trucks, humping water, pulling KP. That how you got hired on at the VA?"

Ajax scrunches his face again. "Why the extra ration of shit? I served. Okay? When did you? Like, World War II?"

Taillights flash across all lanes and Stremmel gives up. He spots an opening and takes it, exiting two offramps early. He has to brake hard at the bottom so as not to run the light. A couple of chairs rattle in the back. Someone yells, "Hey, what the fuck?"

"Sorry," Stremmel says. Then to Ajax, "Word of advice? Don't try and make what you did into something bigger than it was. Not to these guys. They'll have your chow."

He hangs a right on Normandie, goes up a few blocks then takes a left on Artesia Blvd. The van doesn't have GPS, but Stremmel has made the drive plenty of times and knows all the shortcuts when the 405 gets backed up, which it almost always is. He's been working at the VA for 30 years now and has seen guys like Ajax come and go. Most say they quit because of the lousy pay, but Stremmel knows it's because they can't hack working with tadpoles and wheelies day in, day out.

Fast food joints and liquor stores bookend blocks of dingbat apartment buildings and shoebox houses. It's late afternoon and the light's washed out turning everything flat and gray and even though the van's windows are rolled up the air is heavy with the egg stink from a half dozen oil refineries.

"Ah, the smell of what we're fighting for," Ajax says. Stremmel shoots him a look. "What?"

They cross into Torrance and turn into the parking lot of a community college more famous for the alumni who didn't graduate than those who did. Chet Baker, Frank Zappa, Brian Wilson of the Beach Boys. They were all musicians Stremmel grew up listening to, grew up shaped by.

He pulls into a handicap slot. "Game time," he calls out. "Lock and load."

The guys start grunting and griping as they wrestle with the clamps holding down their wheels. "I'll get the ramp and clear the way," Stremmel says to Ajax. "You grab the gear. Bring plenty of towels and the med kit. Whatever you do, don't forget that."

He hits the door button and the electric motor whines as the double doors swing out and the automatic aluminum ramp opens like a switchblade with a bad spring. The ramp's not even all the way down before Banks comes shooting out. "Oorah. Let's get some," he says as his chair bounces onto the pavement.

Banks is always the first one out, the team captain. Was a squad leader, too, never afraid to take point himself, the first guy over the wall, through the door. Most of the guys still wear their hair regulation, but not Banks. His Afro is right out of the '60s even though he wasn't even born then. Stremmel remembers the styles back then, lived them. After his tour in Vietnam he grew a beard and wore a ponytail. Moved north and hid behind the Redwood Curtain for a while, smoking dope, trying to forget. Trading one jungle for another didn't work out so he hitchhiked home and checked himself into the VA. First a patient, now an orderly. With all his seniority, he could have any job at the hospital he wants, but he sticks with SCI patients and LL amputees. His counselor told him it's because he still feels guilty for raking a hootch with his M3 and knocking the legs out from under a half dozen villagers huddled inside. Stremmel can still see them writhing on the mud floor, pictures them grown up, lucky if they ever had a wheelchair, probably nothing better to scoot around on than a scrap of wood nailed to a roller skate. Maybe, he told his counselor, but mostly he just feels more comfortable being around guys with spinal cord injuries and missing legs. "Just the way I roll," he says.

Two co-eds walk by trying not to stare as the guys come wheeling down the ramp. Banks is on them. "Hey, baby, we rolling thunder. Got a lap right here for you. Best seat in the house. Take you anywhere you wanna go. How 'bout it?"

One of the girls cocks her head and puts her hands on her hips. She's got straightened hair and pink fingernails that match her Sketchers. "Uh huh. You better check your tire pressure, playa. You looking a bit flat to me."

Banks makes a big show of clutching his heart as if hit by

an arrow. "You got me, baby. Through and through."

The girls laugh, so does he and keeps on rolling. Banks' biceps bulge beneath the gray hoodie like loaves of bread rising in the oven as he spins his wheels. He wears leather gloves cut off at the knuckles.

Stremmel learned early on never to push a chair without being asked or even to offer. And whenever he is asked, he doesn't expect or get a thank you. But he knows enough to open doors without prompting. The pair leading into the gym are heavy steel and painted battleship gray. He pulls them open and kicks down the rubber stoppers just as Banks rolls up and through. The rest of the men follow in tight formation like a convoy speeding nuts to butts through a sniper alley. Tollson brings up the rear. The peach-fuzz lost both legs below the knee on his first patrol when he stepped on an IED in Helmand Province. Tollson doesn't talk. Stremmel asked the kid's physical therapist about it and she told him he doesn't talk even to his 19-year old wife, and she's a looker, too. "Nothing wrong with his voice box, either. He's got it all bottled up in here," the PT said, tapping the side of her head with a pencil. "Lookout below when he blows."

Banks leads the team across the basketball court to the visitor's bench. They pull off their sweats revealing numbered jerseys. Banks wears a tank top. Tollson's in a longsleeve to cover his arms that are a patchwork of polished skin grafts and corded burn scars. Those with feet have Air Jordan's laced on. As they get ready the captain from the opposing team coasts over. His neck and arms are blued with gang tats. His shoulders are broad, his waist narrow, his legs as skinny and pliant as rope.

"*Que pasa, ese*," he says to Banks.

"Back at ya, brother," Banks says.

They roll close to each other, lean forward, and exchange chest bumps. Both are riding sports chairs with pivoting casters in the front and carbon-spoke racing wheels in the back. The frames are made of titanium. Banks' is painted red, white, and blue. His opponent's candy apple green with a black tuck and roll seat.

Stremmel keeps an eye on the team as he organizes the bench. He takes the gear bag from Ajax and pulls out basketballs and shoots them to the players. Then he sets out water bottles, an orange plastic cooler of Gatorade, and a stack of gym towels. He asks Ajax to hand him the medical kit. The new orderly doesn't respond, he's so busy watching the two teams warming up, dribbling, passing, taking shots. Wheels squeal on the waxed maple boards as players start, stop, and do 360s. Some of the men grunt as they shoot. Footrests clang with each collision.

"They're not half bad," Ajax says.

"Hey, soap for brains," Stremmel says, loud. "What'd you do with the med kit?"

Ajax finally looks his way. "Don't have a heart attack, pops. I couldn't carry it and bring in all the other gear at the same time, now could I?"

"It's still in the van?"

Ajax shakes his head. The gym's fluorescent lights reflect off his shiny scalp. "I dropped it by the front door."

Stremmel blows out some air.

Ajax hooks a thumb at the other team. "They're not vets?"

Stremmel, heading for the door, says over his shoulder, "Slip and falls. Car wrecks. A drive-by or two. Don't underestimate 'em. They won't show any let-up on our guys, for sure."

The med kit is a red duffle bag. Two punks are standing around it. Stremmel elbows past them.

The taller one says, "Hey, old man, what you s'posed to be, some kinda nurse?" He puts his foot on the red duffle. "Who says this your shit?"

Stremmel looks at the shoe stepping on the bag. It's a green LeBron's, $215 a pair. The punk hasn't even bothered to lace it. "Why don't you come in and watch them play?"

The kid curls lips still too young to grow a goatee around. "What for? They don't got game."

"Yeah," the other kid says, grabbing his crotch. "My jack

does more jumpin'." They brush fingertips and bump knuckles.

Stremmel thinks about what he used to say, something like how the players might be cut in half but they'll always be twice the men you punks will ever be. But saying shit like that never changed anything and any good it made him feel only lasted until the next bad spill required him to dress a deep gash in a shin that couldn't even feel the blow. He grabs the straps of the duffle and strips it from under the LeBron's. "We might just surprise you," he says.

Back inside he puts the med kit down next to the rest of the gear. He unzips it so he can reach inside fast when the time comes. Tollson is sitting in front of him, his sweats folded neatly in his lap like a fresh recruit clutching his newly issued uniform waiting for a DI to tell him what to do. Ajax stands next to him holding a paper cup. Gatorade stains his fleshy lips lemon lime. "Looks like the game's starting for real," he says.

The refs are walkers and wear shiny black polyester pants and zebra shirts. A whistle blows and tires screech and chrome roll bars flash. What looks to be a ten car pile-up quickly turns into a sprint as the teams race from one end of the court to the other and back again. Ajax says something about bumper cars and demolition derbies, but Stremmel ignores him as the opening scenes of "Chariots of Fire" start rolling through his head, the actors running barefoot down the beach as the theme song builds and builds. It's the same thing every time, no matter how many games he watches. Stremmel loves that opening scene and song, loved it the first time he saw and heard it, the movie throwing him a life line when it came out, taking the place of an endless loop he couldn't shake no matter how much counseling he got, the over and over again playback of when his squad got caught in their skivvies on the beach at Qui Nhon while Stremmel was showing them how to bodysurf like he used to at Redondo, the ensuing foot chase by a NVA patrol firing their AK's at them, how the sand puffed up like tiny beach umbrellas when the rounds hit around them as they ran, how there was nothing he could do when his buddy from boot went face down, Billy Wagner's bare feet still pumping even though his soles were no longer touching the sand, his eyes no longer seeing.

"Hey," someone shouts. "Hey."

For a moment Stremmel can't tell if it's a line from "Chariots" or his old sergeant yelling at him to keep hauling ass for the jungle. And then he brings it back into focus. "What?"

Ajax is pointing at center court. "Shouldn't we do something?"

Two players are overturned, their topside wheels still spinning, sprawling half in, half out of their chairs. Stremmel knows it's nothing unusual. Players go down all the time and the game rarely stops when they do. Most of the time they right themselves by doing a handspring off the floor or an official tugs them upright. The rulebook doesn't even call for a timeout for a spill unless the player is injured or was blatantly fouled, and even then it's at the discretion of the ref, the chair being considered part of the player. But now the ref is blowing his whistle and the other players are circling their chairs around the downed players. One's Banks.

"You think he's hurt?" Ajax says.

Stremmel tosses him a pair of purple latex gloves. "Bring some towels and plenty of 'em."

He grabs the red duffle and pushes through the chairs circled to block the spectators' view. The ref has already helped the other player up. He's a young Latino from the other team and is pulling the front of his jersey away from his skin. It's wet and a brown smear streaks the front. "*Chingale*," he says. "His shit's all over me."

The team captain with all the tattoos rolls up. "Shut it, *'mano*. Coulda been yours, hey?"

Stremmel drops the med kit and grabs Banks' arm and the still spinning wheel and flips him upright. Then he reaches into the duffle and pulls out an army green poncho, shakes it open, and drapes it over Banks to cover his soiled jersey.

Ajax is there now and staring down at a squished vinyl bag

lying on the court like a roadkill cat. A puddle the consistency of watery mud but isn't spreads across the boards. "Is that what I think it is?"

"Just police it. Dry the floor. They can't restart until you do." Ajax seems frozen so Stremmel barks, "On the double."

Banks wheels off the court and Stremmel hurries behind, the wet soles of his white sneakers squeaking.

"Did your wafer rip off, too?" he asks him.

Banks lifts up the poncho and the dirty jersey underneath. The square baseplate that connects the hole in his intestine to the open end of a colostomy pouch flaps forward, hanging by a corner of its adhesive backing. His stoma is exposed. It's red and puckered and angry looking.

"Yeah. Stung like a motherfucker, too."

Stremmel nods. "Least you can feel something, right?"

Banks' scowl rises at the corners. "Lucky me," he says.

"Hang on. I'll get you back in the game." Stremmel passes him a clean jersey then reaches into the med kit and pulls out a pack of wet wipes, adhesive tape, and a squirt bottle of Purell.

Banks looks over at Tollson, who's still sitting on the sidelines staring off into space. "Roll out, soldier. Squad needs you."

The kid doesn't change expression, just gives both wheels a spin with his palms and heads onto the court. The ref blows his whistle and the game resumes.

Ajax walks up holding a bundle of dirty towels. "What am I supposed to do with these?"

Banks says to Stremmel, "You'd think he picked them up at a Japanese nuclear plant."

Ajax makes a face. "Worst job I ever had? Manning a camp's burn pit in Iraq. You never get the stink of diesel and shit out of your hair."

Stremmel gives Banks a look as if to say, "This is who they send me now."

Shouts come from the court. Tollson is weaving through oncoming defenders like it's a Hollywood car chase scene, one hand spinning a wheel, the other dribbling the ball. The only thing standing at the end of his thousand yard stare now is the basket. When he gets there he makes the perfect layup.

Banks nods in appreciation. "Kid can't talk, but, man, can he handle the rock."

Stremmel finishes cleaning him up, taping down the wafer and screwing on a new vinyl waste pouch. Banks' stomach and chest are zippered with stitch marks, but Stremmel has never asked him what happened. He knows when a guy as gung ho as Banks doesn't tell you what went down, then it had to have been something big and scary and nasty, all right.

"You're good to go," he says, clapping him on the shoulder.

Banks shrugs. "Nah, clock's almost out. Besides, the kid's doing all right. Look at him roll."

The team is passing to Tollson every chance they get. Whatever is chasing him inside his head makes the kid move so fast Stremmel worries his wheels will catch fire. When the buzzer sounds, the vets are up by 10. The teams line up and roll toward each other, slapping skin as they pass. Banks joins in. When he reaches the guy he collided with he doesn't ask for or offer an apology. "Good game," is all he says.

Stremmel turns to Ajax. "Time to pack it up. Let's go."

Ajax is wearing the dopey grin again. "We won. Fucking A, we kicked their ass."

There was a time Stremmel would've said there are no losers in a wheelchair game, that just playing makes them winners, and he would've believed it, too, but now he just zips up the red duffle bag and grabs the Gatorade cooler. "Come on. Move out."

Outside the sun has set, but the darkness isn't that black because of all the cars and the strings of white lights that outline the stacks at the oil refineries like it's Christmas. On the drive home Stremmel stops at a 7-Eleven for a 12-pack of Bud heavies. Cans are passed around in the back. It's against regulation and would cost him his job if they were caught, but as long as he doesn't give in and crack one open himself he's cool with it. He checks the rearview as they get on the 405 southbound to Long Beach. Tollson, clutching an unopened beer can, is staring at the lanes of headlights and taillights streaming by like stripes on a flag.

Back in the VA parking lot the team unloads. Banks wheels over to a black king cab pickup truck with chrome spinners and hoists himself into the driver's seat, pulling his chair up and sliding it into the well behind. He could drive himself to games if he wanted, but he'll always be a squad leader. "Later," he says and takes off. Another player follows in a red Mustang GT. The rest are still inpatients and roll toward the hospital's main entrance staying in tight formation. A silver Jetta idles in the loading zone by the front door. The driver is pretty, not even 20. Her hair is long and blonde and she's watching Tollson hopefully, but he never returns her gaze, his eyes never wavering from the safe cover of the door ahead.

"You can shove off, too," Stremmel tells Ajax.

"You sure?" But the new orderly already has the door open.

"Yeah, I'm sure," he says, as sure as he is that Ajax won't last long on the job.

When he's through parking the rig and checking in the gear Stremmel walks the three blocks home, the sound of traffic droning in the background like the buzz and hum of insects that fill a jungle at night. His studio apartment is on the top floor of a stucco two-story that surrounds a kidney-shaped pool. He opens the sliding glass door and steps out onto the balcony. The landlord put in a gas grill next to the pool and a few of the other tenants are downstairs barbequing burgers and drinking beer. A couple in their swim suits stands in the shallow end talking. They look up and wave, the pale blue water refracting the underwater light, distorting their legs and feet. Stremmel starts to wave back, but then they hop out and walk over to the grill and stand around with the others. Everyone is young, everyone healthy and strong.

He steps back into the apartment and slides the glass door closed and draws the blinds. A half-empty bottle of Jim Beam is on the counter and he pours exactly 120 milliliters into a glass beaker he lifted from the hospital lab and carries it over to a faux leather recliner. He sits and picks up a photograph in a black standup frame from the side table. Eight young men dressed in sweat-stained green fatigues stare back. Some wear helmets, some hold weapons, others cigarettes. Two don't have on shirts, their aluminum dog tags the color of pull tabs. The photo was taken the day before the footrace with the NVA on the beach, before Stremmel raked the hooch soon after. There's Billy Wagner, the sergeant, the rest of the squad with their arms draped around each other's shoulders, some grinning, some just staring. Stremmel's standing in the middle. He's wearing a floppy boonie hat and is looking straight into the camera as if to see into the future. The AP photographer shot it with a Nikkormat that had a light leak so everything from the waist down is ghostlike, fading into white from overexposure.

He cradles the photograph and clicks on a tape deck wired to a pair of bookshelf speakers. The music cues. It's Vangelis. As the opening piano chords fill the room Stremmel sips from the medicine beaker and closes his eyes. All the men he served with and all those he's cared for sprint by, their legs moving as one, their footsteps silent on a beach that never ends.

ABOUT THE AUTHOR

Dwight Holing lives and writes in California. His short stories and essays have appeared in literary journals, including *Arts & Letters*, *Cold Mountain Review*, *Cutthroat*, *Phoebe*, and *Oregon Quarterly*. He is the author of the popular Jack McCoul Capers mystery series. He has written articles for *Audubon*, *Discover*, and *Outside*, among others, and his nonfiction books have been published by Macmillan, Random House, Time-Life, and University of California Press.

Learn: www.dwightholing.com
Follow: @DwightHoling
Like: www.facebook.com/dwight.holing